OUTBREAK

A SURVIVAL HORROR THRILLER

RICHARD DENONCOURT

SELF LAND PUBLISHING

OUTBREAK

BY
RICHARD DENONCOURT

Copyright © 2014 Richard Denoncourt
Self Land Publishing

All rights reserved
version 1.02

Outbreak is a work of fiction. Names, characters, places, and incidents are the products of the author's imagination or are used fictitiously. Any resemblance to actual events, locales, or persons, living or dead, is entirely coincidental.

ALSO BY RICHARD DENONCOURT

TRAINLAND

ASCENDANT

BOOKS IN THE LUMINETHER SERIES

SAVANT: BOOK ONE

FERAL: BOOK TWO

SEER: BOOK THREE

***

The pain in my hand is excruciating.

So this is what it feels like to have your fingernails torn off.

I want to swing my fist into the Colonel's grinning face, but the rope binding me to the table makes it so I can only twitch in helpless rage.

"You gave your word," I manage to growl at him.

The Colonel wipes sweat off my forehead with one hand, a motion almost fatherly in nature. "That I did, brave Kipper. That I did."

He motions for the others to undo my binds. Wheels and Bandanna get to it—grudgingly, I sense from their expressions, but silent as a pair of mimes.

The infected shuffle and moan outside the warehouse. One begins to pound his fist against the wall.

Ignoring them, the Colonel waits for his men to finish. He pulls my gloves out of his back pocket and throws them at me, probably to stanch the bleeding.

"You're going to show me where your stash is," he tells me as I slip on the gloves, wincing at the pain. "That's step number one. Then you're going to enter your humble abode like nothing bad ever happened to you in your whole life.

"Here's the fun part: you're going to come back out carrying your father's head ten minutes after you go in. Not a single minute later. Do you comprehend my vibe, dear Kip? Processing our palaver, so to speak?"

Despite his weird mannerisms, the Colonel's voice is now flat and serious, his face even more so. If this is a game, then it's a totally new level for both of us.

"Or what?" I say. "What happens if I don't come out in ten minutes?"

He leans toward me, clamps his hand around my neck, and draws me close. Our foreheads touch, and I have to endure his nauseating breath.

"Any funny business while you're in that house, Kipper, and I'll inflict so much pain on your little girlfriend that ripping off *her* fingernails will be just the foreplay."

1

ONE DAY EARLIER

After the world fell apart, my father's house became our prison.

He and I were all that was left of my family—maybe all that was left of our town, Peltham Park. And who knew about the world at large? The radio had been dead for years, and the widescreen TV was a shattered relic we used for target practice with our homemade bows and arrows. All we had were our walls, our weapons, and each other.

Which was why, when I found Dad in bed around lunchtime—T-shirt soaked through with sweat, his face the color of ash—I gave in to a crippling panic that froze me in the doorway. That awful word hissed through my mind.

Virus.

It's the virus.

"Dad?"

He opened his eyes with a start, flinching at the slats of light cutting through the boarded window. The blankets were in a twisted pile on the floor. I forced myself to walk over, pick them up, and drape them over him without panicking.

He spoke in a shivering voice, like someone freezing to death.

"It's not what you think, Kip. It's sepsis. You remember how that works?"

"I'm pretty sure," I said, feeling his pulse. "Where's the wound?"

He lifted the blanket, uncovering his right leg, and I saw the dark stain on the lower part of his pant leg.

"I was stupid. I'm sorry, son."

I peeled away the fabric as he explained what happened. He had fallen three days earlier while fixing a hole in the ceiling and had cut his calf on the stone hearth. Lucky it wasn't a broken bone. He'd kept his mouth shut because that's what old, stubborn war veterans like him do. Plus, we had run out of antibiotics the year before, and he didn't see the point in worrying me.

The wound wasn't deep, just a gash he had tried to stitch up on his own. He had done a good job of it, too, but curse bacteria for being so small. I felt hopeless. Three days earlier, we could have made the trek to the pharmacy together, two guns instead of one.

Now I would have to go alone.

"Not happening," he told me. "Don't you dare put a foot outside this house. I mean it."

He was breathing fast. I counted twenty-five breaths per minute. Time was running out, and he would be dead soon. Dead like Mom.

"There's no other choice," I told him.

"There's always a choice," he said. "And I'm not going to let you go."

"You can't stop me."

"God damn it, Kip." He closed his eyes, took a halting breath, and opened them again. "Let's think this through rationally, okay? Going out there is a death sentence. You and I both know that. If you die, I'll die. Let me take my chances. At least you'll live."

I shook my head. "No way. Besides, if you die, I'll have to go out there alone when the supplies run out. Or, I could save your life. Then we could go together."

"But the infected…"

"No point in arguing, Dad. I'm going."

"To *where*?" His voice thickened with anger. "You really think the pharmacy is going to have medicine? After all these years, you think the raiders left it alone because, what, they're doing us a favor? What's the *matter* with you?"

I looked away as he scolded me. I could never look him in the eyes when he got like this, not since I was a kid.

"I'm going," I said in a meek voice.

"Speak up, Kip."

"I said I'm going."

"You understand what could happen to you out there? That those *things* you've only seen from the safety of our roof are the most dangerous predators mankind has ever known? That if you fire a single shot, they'll surround whatever part of town you're in so no matter what direction you run, you can't get through?"

I nodded and looked away again, reconsidering.

"Then why would you go out there?" he asked.

I fought back tears.

"Because I can't let you die, Dad."

Seeing that he was on the verge of protesting again, I got up and turned my back on him. But I couldn't move. I was waiting for him to say the magic words that would keep me from going through with it. What those words might have been, I still don't know.

"You want this," my father said, "don't you."

It didn't sound like a question, so I didn't answer it.

"How long do you have left?" I asked instead.

"Sleep here tonight," he said. "You have to. The dark—"

"How long before it's too late?"

A smacking sound as he tried to swallow with a dry mouth.

"Forty-eight hours," he said. "Sixty, max."

The pharmacy was ten miles away. At a constant walking pace, I could make it there and back in under seven hours. And if I didn't find antibiotics there, I could check houses on the way back.

Plenty of time.

2

I knelt in front of the open closet where we kept the outdoor survival gear and packed my bug-out bag with machine-like intensity. My father had taught me how to do it in the quickest, most efficient way possible. There was an art to it. A perfectly packed B.O.B. was a thing of beauty, except that, unlike a work of art, it could save your life.

He was full of that kind of wisdom, my father—and stories like you wouldn't believe. In the army, he had been a Ranger, and then a Green Beret, and eventually he became a decorated war hero, earning a Bronze Star and a Purple Heart after a mission in Afghanistan in which he took a bullet saving a fellow soldier's life. He had just carried the man out of a burning building when an enemy combatant shot him in the thigh. They both would have died had my father not kept running.

When I trained, I always fantasized about a life in which the Outbreak had never happened, and I was a Green Beret like him.

But on this day, all I could think about was my gear.

Food and water came first. For hydration, I filled a CamelBak with water from our tanks, which were connected by plastic tubes to a discreet collection and filtration system we had built on the roof. Then I dropped a purification tablet into the water and strapped it to my back.

For food, I packed five cans of diced peaches in syrup—sugary enough for a quick energy boost, tinned beans and tomatoes—four of each, and six PowerBars for protein.

"Take three MREs," my father shouted at me from the living room. Earlier, I had helped him move to the couch in front of the hearth.

"MREs"–for the uninitiated—are "Meals-Ready-to-Eat," also known as military rations. They're what soldiers eat during missions, and what lucky survivors get to eat when restaurants and grocery stores have become extinct.

"Not necessary," I shouted back at him. "I've already packed enough calories."

We both knew the truth. Our supply was dwindling. Plus, it was the only food we had left that tasted halfway decent. I would enjoy a few with my father when I got back.

If I got back.

"Kip, God *damn* it, will you listen to me for once? Take three and don't argue."

I let out a quiet sigh before raising my voice again.

"Fine!"

I made a rustling sound in the boxes where we kept them, but didn't actually take any. The extra weight would only slow me down, anyway.

Warmth and protection came next. I donned a fire-resistant Nomex FR Coverall that gloved my entire body, with a zipper in front and buttoned flaps for when nature called. I stuffed a poncho into the extra front pocket of my pack and set aside a rolled sleeping mat to secure to the top when I was done.

I pulled out a pair of never-worn tactical boots—their fresh, leathery scent deliciously thick—and put them on over three pairs of socks. There would be a lot of walking involved. I'd have to avoid the roads entirely in case of raiders, which meant trudging through thick underbrush in wild, overgrown forests.

The inner layer of my pant legs could be tucked into the boots, while the outer layer could slide over the tops to create a protective pocket. Even if I got caught in a heavy rainstorm, my socks wouldn't get wet.

Then came the weapons, my favorite part. I opened one of the shoeboxes containing our limited stock of grenades. There were multiple varieties, all with nicknames my father had picked up in the army: stingers, stunners, flashbangs, smokers, flamers, and of course, your standard-issue, anti-personnel fragmentation grenades. We called them "fraggers."

They had been incredibly difficult to come by. Three and a half years ago, before this part of the country was mobbed with infected, my father and I used to go out in search of "foot markets," which were sort of like black markets but not illegal. These were mobile groups of survivalists like us who used radio communication, Morse code, and other means to gather in secret locations away from raiders and muggers. Most of these people had been in the army, which was how my father gained access to the network. In exchange for things like grenades and automatic weapons, we traded gasoline. It was useless to us since we didn't rely on a generator and had traded our car for MREs.

The grenades were for intimidation in the event someone broke in and posed a threat our guns couldn't handle. My parents and I had decided we would rather blow the place up than let anyone else have it. Otherwise, they were pretty useless—unless you *wanted* to attract every enemy within a five-mile radius.

I left the grenades where they were and moved on.

My father was correct when he said leaving the house was a death sentence, though a more accurate term might have been "suicide." But that only applied to those who went outside unarmed. The rest of us—armed with the proper skills, appropriate gear, and deadliest weapons—still had a fighting chance.

That's what I told myself as I strapped on my holsters and ammo belt.

My father's Glock 17 slid naturally into the holster on my chest, while his black-bladed combat knife went against my right thigh. The knife was for stealth attacks against raiders. Against infected it was useful for everything *but* combat. Getting their blood on your skin was a sure way to catch the virus yourself, so for that reason, I wore a pair of Blackhawk Hellstorm Assault Force gloves made of Kevlar. They were waterproof, couldn't be sliced open, and made gripping and firing a gun seem like the moral thing to do.

Sweating now from the coverall, heart pumping like a piston, I packed two boxes of 9mm ammunition, mostly into the pouches on my belt.

Just two, though. I could have grabbed more, but I didn't. Believe it or not, ammo was near the bottom of useful things to pack. It was heavy, and a gunshot would only attract unwanted attention. Plus, having an abundance of ammo made you feel invincible and less likely to be effective at stealth. To get through this, I would have to be as quick and quiet as possible—a "mouse instead of a lion," my father liked to say (though I preferred a wolf).

Finally, I dug out the list Dad made me promise to look at every time, no matter how well I had memorized it. It would serve to guide me through the next step, and also as a checklist I could use at the very end of the process.

Because the following items were so precious, packing them had to happen at the end. They needed to be easily accessible, which meant inserting them above other items like food and using the pockets and pouches on my coverall and utility belt.

The items on the list were as follows: four emergency bottles of water (one went into my belt), a Zippo lighter, a clamshell mirror (for scouting around corners), waterproof matches, a tactical LED flashlight, a set of lock picks that included a glass cutter the size of a pencil and suction cups for gripping glass, a Leatherman multi-tool, waterproof binoculars with 8.5x magnification and 45mm objective lens, a lightweight axe for chopping through boards (which also went on my belt), and a twelve-foot, twisted-fiber climbing rope with a grappling hook at one end, for climbing those hard-to-reach places. I strapped on a wrist compass and packed a navigation kit that included topographical maps of Peltham Park and its surrounding towns.

I was forgetting something.

I opened a desk drawer and took out the lucky rabbit's foot my mother had given me before she died. I kissed it before slipping it into a pouch on my belt.

A pop sounded in the living room. I almost ran to my father, convinced he had shot himself to make me stay. Then I heard another pop, followed by a dry crackle.

The fireplace. He must have lit it for warmth.

"You look good," he said when I emerged carrying all my gear.

He was just lowering himself back to the couch, panting from the exertion.

"Thanks," I said. "Any last-minute tips?"

"Keep your ammunition dry. Strip your pistol and clean it before you—"

"I already did. Yesterday."

"What? How the hell did you know—"

"I clean it every day, Dad. You know that."

"Right, right. You and your hobbies."

He tried to swallow, but his mouth was too dry. I picked up the water bottle I had left on the coffee table, unscrewed it, and made him take a few swallows.

"I'll be back soon," I said. "All the water and food you need is on the armchair."

I tilted my head in the direction of the small pile I had built on the cushion. Would he have the strength five hours from now to make his way over there and tear open an MRE or a PowerBar wrapper? If he could light the fire, then he could probably feed himself—but not for much longer.

"You bringing the assault rifle?" he asked me.

"I shouldn't need it."

"Good," he said. "Too loud. Plus, you and that Glock were meant for each other. But it won't be like firing off the roof with a silenced rifle, all right? Once you're down there and staring one of those bastards in the eye, it's a whole different ballgame. You need to be sure. The noise..."

A sudden coughing spell made him curl up and shake. I gave him more water. My muscles were tense. Time was running out.

"I'm going," I said. "I love you."

"Love you, too, Kip. Be careful, and be fast. If you don't find anything, come home. Don't linger. Every minute that goes by is..."

He didn't finish. His strength had left him. He closed his eyes and drifted into sleep.

I kissed his forehead before making my way to the door leading into the garage and quickly undid the complex system of locks and bolts. I put as much of it back together as I could on the other side. Of course, the locks wouldn't hold against a few well-placed shots. But the real fortifications had been built into the outer layers of the house.

It was dark inside the garage. I used the Zippo to cast a shivering glow over the workbench and the busted minivan. A moldy, musty smell hung in the air. There were tools and parts everywhere, lying all over the floor, covered in dust that seemed ancient.

The garage doors had been reinforced with sheet metal and steel beams in case a group of infected came up with the idea of ramming into them. We had done such a good job of it that, in the dim light, the doors looked like gaping holes—tunnels leading God only knows where, full of lurking dangers.

I made my way quickly to the hatch where a window used to be. Seconds later, I was outside.

3

Trash speckled the high grass of the yard and covered the length of our street. I had seen it plenty of times from the roof, but from down here, it almost looked as if a giant party had been thrown across the entire neighborhood, and no one had bothered to clean up afterward.

I picked up one of the rolled newspapers still in its plastic delivery shell and tried to check the date. The paper was little more than oatmeal now. I tossed it aside and chided myself for wasting time. Checking my wrist compass, I headed toward the trees.

It had rained recently. The full, vibrant smell of wet forest caught me off guard with its delicious thickness. A smell I'd forgotten existed. As I breathed it in, I pulled out my navigation kit.

One of the survival techniques my father had drilled into me over the years was how to shoot an azimuth. That's when you determine the line between you and an object in the landscape you want to reach—in my case, the Super-Mart on Route 1—using a topographical map and a compass. I was twelve years old the first time he taught me, and I'll never forget it.

That was before the Outbreak, so I never actually thought I'd use it. But my father had been adamant and made me practice every weekend for a whole summer, and then again the summer after that. Either he wanted me to join Special Forces, or he knew the world was doomed. I became as familiar with a compass as the jocks in my school had been with throwing a baseball. Not that it got me any attention from girls, unfortunately.

I became so good with it that on a camping trip near the mountains one summer, my father decided to give me the ultimate test.

"When I did this in the army," he said, passing me a nav kit, "we called it 'the Star.'"

The wonder in his voice made it seem like a mythical test originally given to a Greek hero. I went along without complaint, eager to please, not even asking for details.

He took off alone at dawn the following morning and set up a tent somewhere in the forest. When he returned hours later, he marked the tent's location on my map and made me walk to it alone, through miles of wooded terrain, counting every step to gauge the distance according to my measurements on paper.

I had failed that time, and I failed this time, too. I got lost.

After shooting a couple more azimuths to get myself on track, I made it through the forest and onto a road I recognized. What should have taken two hours ended up taking four. Stinging pain on the pads of my feet told me I'd have blisters pretty soon, despite my three layers of socks. I cursed myself for not having broken in my boots sooner. Rookie mistake.

Plenty of time, I kept telling myself. *I have plenty of time. Unless the pharmacy is empty.*

A quick dinner of canned peaches and a PowerBar silenced my churning stomach. I followed a familiar road for the next hour, using my binoculars to see ahead. It was a desperate shortcut, but I needed to make up for lost time. I would have been amazed if raiders had set up a trap in such a quiet area. Nothing I had seen so far indicated those evil bastards even came up this way.

I arrived into town five and a half hours into my journey, at around six thirty. Thankfully, it was early spring, which meant the daylight would keep for another hour. Darkness in a land full of mindless, deliriously hungry cannibals was a scary thing. Scarier still was the knowledge that I would have to make camp at some point. There was no way I would try and brave the darkness.

Plenty of time. I've got plenty of time.

"Finally," I said, looking into my binoculars at a sight I hadn't laid eyes on in three years.

The commercial part of Peltham Park, located along Route 1, had once been a bustling strip of outlet malls, restaurants, and banks. Not the sort of gaudy and colorful McDonald's-and-KFC-infested mess you might find closer to Boston, but a neat arrangement of New England-style buildings that held mid-sized supermarkets, lobster joints, and the occasional Home Depot. Even the sprawling outlet malls had tasteful facades that complemented the flavor of the town.

Now, however, it was a cluster of dilapidated shells riddled with broken windows and crude graffiti, the parking lots empty except for the trash. The graffiti is what bothered me most. With the rest of mankind facing a grim and bloody fate, the thought of a bunch of assholes spray-painting the walls of my town was enough to make my trigger finger restless.

The closer I got, the more unsettled I became. I had expected this kind of desolation—broken windows and all—but not the spray-painted messages. Some of them said things like "WE DESERVED IT" and "GOD FUCKED US FINALLY." Worthless, defeatist crap.

I also didn't expect the naked body, now little more than a skeleton, hanging from a streetlamp near the intersection, or the charred remains of a dentist's office someone had obviously torched. It made the prospect of finding medication at the town pharmacy feel like the naïve fantasy of a kid who still believes in treasure maps.

But at least I wasn't sitting home doing nothing, just watching my father die like I did with Mom.

I came to the parking lot of an outlet mall shaped like an L. There had been a dozen stores here once. Now there were only six ruined facades guarding empty spaces. If I was going to set up camp somewhere for the night, probably one of those buildings would be best. But with a steely gray light still in the sky, and the pharmacy so close, I pressed forward, keeping south in the hope of making up for lost time.

Some of the buildings I passed triggered memories so pleasant I knew savoring them would only hurt afterward. One of them was Tommy's Bike Shack. In my early teens, I had been obsessed with bicycles. I would go to Tommy's every weekend to top off the air in my tires and listen to the repair guys talk about gear and upcoming biking trips. My best friends at the time, Tom Brand and Mike Culliver, would ride there on the weekends to meet me, and together the three of us would take off to parts as yet unexplored, where we could lay down our special brand of harmless mischief (mostly petty vandalism and drinking booze stolen from our parents' liquor cabinets).

I snuck around the building. A quick glance through a back window told me there wasn't much inside. I saw what looked like bicycle chains, two or three, spilled across the floor, and other supplies I didn't need.

Twenty minutes later, I passed the back deck of a small restaurant—The Brass Lantern—where I had bussed tables my freshman year of high school. The former restaurant was falling apart, but I stopped for a moment to visualize its quaint appearance back when I had been a fifteen-year-old kid making five bucks an hour, plus ten percent of the tips earned by the waitresses. One of them, a stooped old lady named Hilda, had once tried to explain the rules of Bridge to me on an unusually slow Saturday night. Half-listening, I had devoted most of my attention to one of the other waitresses—Joanna Rushforth—and what she must have looked like without clothes.

I still wonder, though I'm sure Joanna is dead.

A GROUP of them had gathered in the parking lot of a Citizens' Bank.

By then, I had seen enough infected—usually of the lone-wolf variety—from the roof of my house that I was able to ignore the group for a moment and study the area around them. I noticed several things, like how the drive-up ATM machine had been utterly destroyed, and how the bank's front door no longer existed. So far, it seemed all the buildings along Route 1 had either been looted, destroyed by infected, or both. This didn't bode well for my mission.

The group was mostly made up of men, but there were a few women with ragged hair that hung past their shoulders in filthy strips. I counted twelve altogether. They shuffled around with their heads lolling to one side. Now and then, one would trip and fall, or bump into another, inciting a groan of protest. A couple of the more gray-skinned ones, clearly in the late stages of infection, had gone blind and swung their arms around as if swatting at imaginary wasps.

They looked harmless, but I knew the truth. Groups were dangerous and to be avoided at all times. If the wind turned, and they caught a whiff of my scent, I'd end up in a really unfortunate situation.

I was about to get going when the dull roar of an engine rose nearby. I tightened my grip on the Glock and listened. The infected also heard the noise—no surprise there, considering how loud the damned thing was—and tilted their heads like dogs. A bunch snarled and bared their teeth. A few of the stronger ones fell into attack postures, ready to pounce on any healthy human that entered their field of vision.

The vehicle appeared, and I was stunned by what I saw. It was a muddy Jeep Wrangler with four men inside. It tore into the parking lot as if on a mission to attract the most infected possible.

The driver was a skinny guy with the wild appearance of a mountain man. Next to him, another guy stood in the passenger seat. He leaned against the open frame, wearing a red bandanna that was now almost pink with age. The Jeep came to a sudden stop. Bandanna aimed an automatic rifle at the infected but didn't shoot as they shuffled toward the vehicle. He was waiting.

There were two other men in the Jeep. In the back seat, a thickset guy with oiled, wavy black hair and a bushy black beard held a pistol to the temple of a more muscular man seated next to him. The muscular guy had a shaved head and looked like an ex-convict. He also looked terrified.

I watched with growing alarm as the man with the black beard stood up suddenly, lifted the ex-con-looking guy, and tossed him out of the Jeep.

He screamed as the infected tore into him. The two men in the front of the Jeep smiled at the carnage, the driver even chewing gum as he watched. The one in the back seat just stared in admiration at his own work.

I recognized him—the guy with the bushy black beard who had performed the execution.

Still standing, he rested his bearish, tattooed forearms on the Jeep's frame. He had a neck tattoo that revealed itself as he craned his neck to say something to the driver. With a nod, the driver blew out his gum and sent it into the frenzied pack. He cut the wheel, floored the gas pedal, and left behind a cloud of dust as he tore out of the parking lot.

It was the neck tattoo that triggered my memory of him. An unusual design, it was a rendering of black roses attached to a thorny stem—except the stem was made of barbed wire. Realistic shading on the skin made the wire appear to dig into it. The design was wicked; tall enough to run along the underside of his chin, it bloomed black roses along its entire length, at least a dozen of them.

And here's your change, good sir, the man had said to me—not quite a British accent, but more the voice of a man with more personality than he can contain.

He had been a cashier at the Exxon station just down the street. Before the Outbreak, I used to pass the store on my drive home from soccer practice and sometimes swing in to buy an energy drink if I had to pull an all-nighter for school.

He had been a talkative guy back then. More than once,

he had informed me that too many Red Bulls could screw up my kidneys. We got on a first-name basis, though I forget his name now after so many years. I used to wonder about his black-rose-and-barbed-wire tattoo, and whether or not he was one of those ex-cons working a shitty hourly job as a way to reintegrate with society. He just had one of those looks that said "prison."

After what I had just seen in the Citizens' Bank parking lot, I was probably right about the prison thing. I put away the binoculars and readied myself for the next leg of my journey. Hopefully I would never cross paths with the guy again.

Or his neck tattoo might end up being the last thing I'd ever see.

4

What follows is a true account of my three days and two nights in Peltham Park.

For those interested in how I survived after a half dozen others had to die, go ahead and continue reading. Maybe you're a historian or social scientist fascinated with what we now call the "Hunger Virus" era. Or you've grown up sheltered and crave a sense of adventure you can only get from books.

There's also the possibility that no one will read this manuscript, and putting down these words is just my way of trying to cleanse my mind of the nightmares that wake me up each night—the ones where I'm covered in sweat, raking in each breath, and thinking there's blood all over my hands.

Blood of my father that I could have sworn I washed off years ago.

In my memory of that time, I'm just a scared twenty-year-old kid whose entire life is about to change in ways he never imagined—and it begins with a mistake I make the very first night.

IT'S TIME TO REST, even though I could go further.

Night has fallen and the buildings of Peltham Park are black against a purple, glittering sky. There isn't a single light anywhere except the millions of stars above. Empty shells of old cars squat in the dark, dimly reflecting the cosmic glare, each one a sad reminder of movement, destinations, progress. In the distance, a wolf emits a lonesome howl that makes me think of the wilderness that was here when the first settlers arrived.

With the entire town abandoned, it's easy to waste thought energy on this kind of nonsense.

I've reached my destination, the old SuperMart on Route 1 where my mother had once picked up her medication. Crouched behind the building, which is part of a connected row of stores, I'm thinking this is the end of the line for now. I can't go any farther, not without daylight. Dawn is maybe eight hours away.

Plenty of time, I tell myself.

The time, though, my inner voice sounds like it's mocking me.

A nearby Dumpster tipped onto its side should serve pretty well as a shelter for the night. It lies with its opening facing a concrete divider. I manage to quietly move it a few inches so the lid can rest on the barrier, forming a roof of sorts. I rotate the Dumpster with one corner touching the concrete wall, leaving only one narrow opening to serve as an entrance; then I crawl in and spread my sleeping mat so my head will lie opposite the opening. That way, if one of them reaches inside, it'll grab my boot before any other part of me. It smells god-awful in here, though I can tell the years have removed the worst of it.

I keep the pistol close to me, along with the tube attached to my Camelbak, in case I wake up and need to have a drink. I also keep an empty plastic bottle nearby in case I have to urinate in the middle of the night.

I close my eyes and listen to the sound of the wind as it carries the moans of infected moving along Route 1.

I dream about my mother.

Several times during the night I wake up in that foul-smelling darkness thinking I'm back in the house with her and Dad. I have trouble remembering the dreams that wake me, but I know they're the same ones that have haunted me since she died. Dark dreams in which my mother sits across from me in various unlit rooms of our house, and though neither of us moves or speaks, I can tell she is slowly losing her mind. I know by the way she stares at me through black eyes like holes in her skull.

FOR ALMOST TWO years after the Outbreak, Mom and Dad were the only two people in my life—not just the only two I loved, but the only people I had any contact with whatsoever. Despite this closeness, my father and I didn't know about Mom's addiction until it was too late.

Painkillers. They had been her drug of choice, her way of finding peace. I remember seeing her sprawled on the couch most days, wearing her pajamas and staring at nothing. She kept the source of her daily stupors hidden from us. We thought she was depressed, but then again, my father and I were spending twelve hours a day training and fortifying the house. We were shocked when we found out the truth.

On rare good days, when she was lucid and in a bouncy mood, Mom would don her apron and cook for us. We ate using the fine silver, the white, precious china, and the crystal glasses. If something broke, we laughed about it. When we felt like splurging, we would dip into our stock of batteries and run the portable stereo. My dad and I would swing my mother around the living room to the music of Ray Charles and other Fifties greats. Or we would listen to Frank Sinatra and reminisce. Eric Clapton was too much for Mom and always made her cry.

The day she began to turn was one of the worst of my entire life. It was my father's paranoia that saved his life and mine.

"Where were you?" he asked my mother.

Mom had just come in through the emergency hatch we had built in the back of the house, the one that couldn't be opened from the outside. She'd had to knock to be allowed back in. We hadn't even seen her leave.

"I went next door," she said, slurring her speech. "It's no big deal, hon."

My father checked her pockets and found the painkillers. The prescription had been made out to one of our neighbors.

"They were dead," my mother said. "In bed. Dead in bed. He shot her and then himself. Shot her and then himself. Dead in bed."

She had walked there and back wearing no shoes, which supported my theory that she had already begun to lose her mind even before catching the virus. There was dried blood on her feet.

"Honey," my father said. "Sweetheart. What did you step on? Are you cut? Tell me where the blood came from, Jessica."

My mother smiled and said in a girlish voice, "Stepped on a bedbug. Dead in bed."

I had never seen my father cry until that moment. Tears streamed down his face as he ordered me to my room.

We locked her in my parents' bedroom, where we could only see her by looking through the keyhole. The room was always dark, even in the day. More often than not, she was little more than a silhouette in the lines of sunlight slicing through the boarded windows.

Sometimes Mom just sat there and pulled out her hair. Other times, she would snarl and tear at the mattress, or jostle the backboard like she was trying to pull it out.

I don't know why I watched. One morning, I found her only inches away from the keyhole, one eye narrowed as she tried to see me through it. Her face was covered in red slashes, most of her hair already missing.

"Kip," she said in a harsh whisper. "Is that you? Did you put the trash out?"

My father used his Desert Eagle. He waited until she was in a state of fitful sleep. By that point, she rarely slept soundly, if at all. He opened the door, walked in, and closed it shut behind him. I sat at the piano, running my fingers over the keys without pressing them, listening and waiting for it to be over.

He took an enormous risk in leaving the house to bury her. I spent that whole day waiting for him, convinced he wasn't coming back. When he finally did, we made dinner, then spent the evening talking about the things we loved most about her. We cried and talked for hours, then agreed not to speak of her again. She was in the past, like the rest of the world we had once known. Survivors didn't live in the past.

And just like that, we moved on.

. . .

DAYLIGHT, finally.

I haven't slept more than a few hours. My body is stiff, and my mouth tastes like the Dumpster smells. I eat a quick breakfast—peaches and a Powerbar—before sliding out of my little shelter to seek cover in a grove of trees nearby. I don't make the mistake of assuming I'm alone.

But I am—for now, anyway.

The town is pale blue and quiet in the early morning light. This time of day always makes me nostalgic, and I think of days past even as I tell myself to pay attention. My heart sinks with each step I take toward the SuperMart.

The place has been ransacked. That much is clear from the broken windows and the debris all over the parking lot. And yet I entertain the possibility that the inside has been left untouched. There are infected all over the front parking lot, and maybe, just maybe, their presence has been enough to keep away raiders and scavengers all these years.

The chances of that are slim.

On a positive note, the infected aren't formed in groups. I count close to thirty scattered across the small lake of concrete, all standing apart from each other. Even from this distance, I can smell their dank clothes and unwashed, putrid bodies. Their rotting heads droop forward and their necks are a vile shade of red from burning in the sun.

A woman stumbles around in a circle, arms jerking as if she is conducting an orchestra that exists only in her own diseased mind. In the distance, a skinny man dressed all in black wrestles with a toppled shopping cart that must be from the grocery store at the opposite end. Most of the infected are just standing there or shuffling around aimlessly.

The grocery store. I forgot there was one here. Maybe it'll have—

But any urge to explore it dissolves when I see the gaping black hole where the entrance used to be. It looks like someone backed a garbage truck through it.

I make my way around the strip of buildings. The Super-Mart has a set of three loading bay doors in the back. I take it as a good sign that none of them is busted or covered in graffiti. Above them is a ledge that extends a few feet from the windows, which are surprisingly intact. I take out my grappling hook and toss it up. When it finally catches, I test it a few times before shimmying up the rope.

The storm windows are made of impact-resistant glass, difficult to break without making a lot of noise. I use the glasscutter to cut a rectangular opening, and the suction cups to pull out the glass so I can quietly set it aside. Once I'm through, I find myself in an office that has been trashed, a place so quiet I almost expect to hear the beep of a computer.

It looks like hell in here, but there is no sign that raiders or scavengers have been through. I allow myself a few seconds to bask in a pleasant, hopeful feeling.

Out in the dank, unlit hallway, I come to a featureless gray door on which my flashlight reveals two signs, one stating "Employees Only" beneath another that reads "FIRE ESCAPE" with the universal symbol for stairs. First turning off my flashlight to avoid drawing attention, I open the door. Of course, the stairwell beyond is completely dark. I catch a whiff of infected. It's light, just a fringe smell, which means the stairs are probably empty. I crouch in the darkness, close my eyes, and listen anyway.

Not a thing. I decide it's safe to turn on my flashlight and make my way down, my senses on full alert, the flashlight's beam stretching shadows on the wall. When I reach the bottom of the stairs, I turn it off and peek out the door to the shopping area.

The store looks twice as big as I remember, though that's probably an illusion caused by the shelves, most of which have been toppled. My chest expands with hope when I see that the shelves against the wall still contain various supplies, like toilet paper and toothbrushes.

If raiders had been through here, they wouldn't have left behind such luxuries. There's a possibility that only infected —who have no desire for such things, including medicine— are the only people to have come through this store since the town fell.

My hopes dwindle as one of my father's favorite lessons runs through my mind.

If it seems too good to be true, then it probably is. Play devil's advocate eighty percent of the time, in a hundred percent of situations.

Okay, Dad. Fine. There's a distinct possibility that raiders *have* been through here, and that they took so many supplies they either couldn't fit everything, or they could afford to leave behind things like toothbrushes.

If that's true, medicine is one of the first supplies they would have grabbed. I might be shit out of luck.

The front half of the store is well-lit thanks to the broad windows. A dozen or so infected loiter there. From my spot in the darkened back area, I'm well hidden from any that might glance in my direction. Of course, the store's back half could hold just as many infected as the front, or more, hiding in the shadows. As my eyes adjust to the darkness, I see a few of them among the shelves, but they seem intent on whatever it is they're doing. Playing with the store's remaining wares, probably.

The pharmacy is right where I remember it. There are no windows along its back wall because the loading area is behind it. No windows means no light, and I already consider the possibility that the space is filled with infected, and that taking out my flashlight to read the labels might be too dangerous to attempt.

I approach the long counter serving as a border between the pharmacy and the rest of the store. Keeping to the shadows, I lean over the counter and peer inside. I see empty shelves in the low light, but that doesn't mean the place has been cleaned out. Maybe the bottles were knocked over by infected.

I look down at the floor and see small, pale, uniform shapes. My heart soars.

Medicine.

5

When I'm sure no infected are looking my way, I carefully slide over the counter. I keep low to the ground, my hands feeling the bottles to make sure they're not just empties. But the lids are screwed on tight and I can hear pills clicking around inside.

A flashlight would really help right now, but it's too risky. With no other light back here, the beam would be easy to spot.

Every problem has a solution, however—especially when you bring the right tools.

I take out the Leatherman multi-tool and click on the tiny blue bulb on one of its prongs. The light isn't strong enough to guide someone through a dark room, but it's perfect for reading the labels.

I've taken care of the lighting situation, but that was the easy part. Now I have to deal with the noise. The sporadic moaning and growling of the infected on the main floor might mask the clicking of the pills. But I can't risk finding out the hard way.

A loud thump from the shopping area startles me. The

noise is followed by a series of angry snarls. I raise my head to peer over the counter, just in time to see two infected wrestling in the central aisle. They must have tripped over each other. After a few seconds of kicking and pushing, one gets up, a black shape against the glare from the windows, and makes its way toward the front as if nothing happened. The other rolls over a few times but doesn't get up.

With a relieved breath, I go back to work.

There's only one way to keep silent, and it requires moving around on all fours without touching the bottles I don't need. I keep the multi-tool between my clenched teeth and make my way over the mess, careful to place my hands and boots on bare sections of the floor. It's incredibly difficult to do, and I move with the slowness of a turtle—a fitting image since my pack weighs oppressively against my spine.

I've studied my father's survivalist manuals and medical journals enough to know what kinds of medication apply to my current situation. The virus isn't the only infection people like us need to worry about. The other silent killer is bacterial.

Which is why I'm incredibly lucky to find a full bottle of Nafcillin followed by, mere minutes later, a bottle of Vancomycin. Both are industrial size, each containing five hundred pills. But there's enough space in each bottle to make carrying them around as noisy as shaking a pair of maracas.

I find a spot between two shelves, slide off my pack, and get to work opening the bottles and stuffing them with toilet paper. (I forgot to mention I packed that as well—should be no surprise there.) Once they're both full, I screw on the caps. Then I test the noise level by tapping them against my thigh.

Barely a click of sound. I stuff them into the bottom of

my pack, so they won't fall out or get in the way, then slide my pack forward to clear a bit of room for my legs, which I stretch to avoid cramps.

A good idea would be to search the place for more valuable medicine. But just as I start to push myself off the ground, a metallic click makes me freeze.

It can't be what I think it is—can it?

I reposition myself into a crouch, close my eyes, and listen. The ensuing shuffling sound that rises to my left is slow and clumsy, as if the intruder is uncertain about entering all the way. A sour, fleshy smell thickens the air— not quite the smell of rot, but close.

Early-stage infected. Somehow it managed to open the pharmacy's side door. It was stupid of me not to check it first.

Now the only question is: how many are there?

Sudden silence tells me the thing has stopped walking. I'm thankful for the shelf blocking me from view, though it won't help if the smell of my sweat gives me away. I listen more closely and hear a sniffing sound.

The most important thing—besides avoiding contamination—is keeping my pack with me at all times. Without it, I'm a dead man and so is my father.

It's bad luck, I guess. The pack lies with its bulging bottom extending past the shelf. If I try to move it, the infected will see the motion.

There is nothing of interest to them inside my bag. I could leave it here and come back, and there's a good chance they'll leave it alone since it doesn't smell like food and is very tough to open, especially with hands connected to a virus-eaten brain like theirs.

Again, I hear the shuffling sound of movement, along with vocal sounds. There are two of them, each making a distinct noise—a male emitting a low moan, and a woman letting out a thin whine that sounds like air leaking from a balloon.

Unless I consider jumping over the counter a viable means of escape—which it isn't because I can't see what's on the other side—there is really only one option, and that's the door. The problem is the two infected standing in the way. Could I use the knife to take them out quietly? It's possible, but the risk is too great. If I attract a swarm, I'll never get out.

A desperate idea comes to me.

I reach down to one of the pouches hanging off my belt. The moans and footsteps grow louder as the infected approach my position, only seconds away from appearing in front of me. I slide a few fingers into the pouch, wrap them around the Zippo, and slip it out.

I flip the lid back, snap my thumb against the flint wheel, and watch the spark fatten into a shivering flame half an inch tall. I flick it into the far corner. By the time it lands, there is nothing hiding me from the infected. The male could have turned and easily caught me sitting there.

Instead, the flame catches their attention. They lunge at it. The medicine bottles are a lucky trap, and the infected lose their footing and collapse in a tangle.

I grab my pack and sprint past the door. As effective as my plan ended up being, it caused enough racket to draw every infected person in the SuperMart—and even a bunch from outside—toward the pharmacy. Dark shapes fill the front windows.

Running in a low crouch, I make my way to the stairwell. I take the steps two at a time and emerge unscathed in the same dank hallway as before. My flashlight cuts a tunnel through the darkness.

I'm safe for now. But something is wrong. It smells different in here—rank body odor combined with a dry, papery smell unlike anything an old office would emit.

Pulse pounding in my ears, I hold the Glock and the flashlight side by side in both hands as I creep forward. The room with the windows should be right around the corner. I can use the grappling hook to climb back down. Shouldn't take more than three minutes to be on my way.

But that *smell*.

What could it be? The papery and spicy nature of it reminds me of a dried wasp's nest, only several times more pungent, and mixed with something like armpit odor.

I no longer need the flashlight and click it off before rounding the corner. The trashed office is to my left, daylight streaming through the open door. It hits me full-on in the face and makes me wince.

A dry-sounding bark almost makes me fire the pistol into the darkness at the other end of the hallway. Instead, I aim straight ahead at where I expect my attacker's chest to be. When they emerge—two males down on all fours—I adjust my aim, but it's too late.

They charge me like a pair of chimpanzees, feet banging the carpeted floor.

Skinny, hairless, and covered in dust—more like monsters than anything human.

I'm too freaked out to aim properly and shoot. Instead, I leap out of their way and land inside the office. As they lunge past the door, I catch a glimpse of pale skin stretched over ribs, emaciated arms covered in scratches, and then a pair of ghastly, skeletal faces that whip around to study me through the doorway.

Two sets of milky eyes blink at me. I was wrong about them both being males.

It's actually a man and a woman, though it's hard to tell the difference since they both seem to weigh about ninety pounds and have lost all hair including their eyebrows. Both are shirtless and barefoot, though the man wears tattered jean shorts and the woman a pair of torn spandex pants. So many old scars and fresh cuts decorate the exposed parts of their bodies that it's like they drew maps all over each other with a razor blade, etching new features over the ones that had healed. The fine layer of dust covering them must be from the plaster used in the construction of these offices, meaning they've been trapped in here a while.

I extend my boot, hook it behind the door, and kick it shut in their faces. I'm up in a flash and immediately twist the lock in the doorknob to seal it shut. The two infected waste no time. They pound the door with such force that I reconsider just how strong late-stagers can be.

When they start hammering the sheets of Plexiglass in the windows facing the hallway, I know I'm in trouble. The glass holds for about three seconds before falling inward with a bang that sends sheets of paper fluttering. Like a couple of pale frogs, the man and the woman leap through the opening and land inside the office.

There's no time to climb back outside. I face the emaciated couple. Sure enough, they're both wearing gold wedding bands.

Married.

These two loved each other once. Maybe they still do.

None of that stops me from aiming the Glock at their chests, and yet I can't pull the trigger. They don't look hungry or violent or even angry at being disturbed. They just blink in my direction with red-veined, milky eyes.

I shouldn't have hesitated. They duck at the same time, movements perfectly in sync. I fire at empty air. The pop is deafening. They spring toward me with surprising agility and tackle me to the ground.

The gun slips out of my hand. I would pick it back up, but all four of my limbs are suddenly occupied in the struggle to fend them off. On my left side, the man struggles to bite into my raised forearm, but the coverall's fabric keeps me protected. The woman is more vicious and tries to claw at my face. I resist using my right arm and slam my leg into her side with enough force to roll her off.

The man's teeth snap above my face. A line of drool swings from his cracked lower lip. If a single fleck enters my mouth or one of my eyes, I'm toast.

The woman scrambles to get back up. When she finally does, I manage to locate the pistol lying next to me. I sweep my arm over it and slide it closer to my hip, where I can finally grab it. The woman readies herself to pounce, and I use the opportunity to aim at her chest.

As I'm about to shoot, a strange thing happens.

Her head jerks forward as if she's been punched. When she lifts it again, I see an arrow that wasn't there before. It entered through the back and impaled her left eye as it emerged through the front, destroying enough of her brain to drop her. Who could have shot that thing so perfectly?

I can't let the mystery of the arrow distract me, not with my left side pinned beneath the man's weight. His mouth is leaking spit like a faucet. A gob of it lands next to my head, and I catch the cheesy smell coming from his rotten, yellow tongue.

The Glock. I need to use the Glock.

I push him away at an angle to distance myself from his toxic saliva. There's just enough space between us now that I can press the Glock's barrel to his ribcage.

The shot sends a jolt through my entire body, but it's

nothing compared to what it does to the man. He jolts upright with a gasp, paws at the wound, and starts to spin, his mouth gaping open in a silent scream.

I put another bullet in his skull. Then I do the same to the woman, though it's clear she isn't getting back up again. Another glimpse of the arrow sticking through her head reminds me I'm not alone in the room.

I swing around, pistol raised, and fall instinctively to one knee in the case the archer has loosed another arrow at me. But this mystery archer is actually a young woman, and though she aims what appears to be an expensive bow at me, I can tell by the guarded, fearful look in her eyes that she doesn't want to shoot.

I lower the pistol. The room goes quiet except for the sound of our breaths. I'm sure every infected within a hundred yards heard the gunfire and is making a beeline toward the SuperMart. The girl's eyes lock with mine, and I know she's thinking the same thing.

And yet, despite the urgency of our situation, all we can do is stare at each other. I don't know what to think. Armed with a small pack, an arrow quiver, and a utility belt, she wears a coverall almost identical to mine, except hers is Navy Blue whereas mine is black. There's no doubt she's a trained survivalist, but the way her nostrils flare with each breath, and the unblinking fear in her eyes tell me she's having trouble accepting this situation.

"Kip?" she says. "Is that really you?"

I'm stunned.

"How—how do you—"

The words catch in my throat. Suddenly I'm convinced this is some sort of trick. I've heard stories over the years—at first on the radio and then from my father—of raiders who enlist or force young women to lure unsuspecting survivors into traps.

But even if that's the case, how in the hell does she know my name?

"Relax," the girl says. "We went to school together."

I loosen up a bit. Maybe if she wasn't so grimy, I would have been able to recognize her. Now that I think about it, I've seen her face before; only it looks slightly different because of the weight she's lost in the past several years. Her name is Marie or something like it.

"Peltham Park High School," I say. "You were in the class below me."

She nods slightly, eyes locked on mine. I wonder why she doesn't blink.

"Can I trust you?" she says.

"I was wondering the same thing. Marie, right?"

"Melanie."

She says it quickly with no sign she's offended by my slip up. I never knew her in high school, but her name is familiar—and mine, too, probably—from posters the school drew up when she and I both ran for president of our respective classes. She was elected. I wasn't.

"Melanie, listen to me," I say. "They're coming. The infect—"

"I know, I know. We need to get out of here. But how?"

"The window," I say, gesturing to the hole I cut into the glass. "I have a grappling rope we can use. We'll figure out the rest later."

She hurries past me and climbs through the window. I can't help but wonder what makes her trust me so easily. In a world like this, a guy my age is more likely to be a rapist or a thief than a normal guy.

"This way," she says when we're on the ground.

I gather the rope and follow her southward.

South. Even though my house is to the north.

We crouch-run along Route 1, using what cover we can find along the way to avoid exposing ourselves. We're headed toward a Lubroline station a half-mile away.

"I can't stay," I tell Melanie.

"Just be quiet."

I follow her, shaking my head. This is so stupid. My father is going to die, and it'll be my fault, all because of a girl. How can I be sure she isn't leading me into a trap?

"Wait," I say, grabbing her arm and pulling her into a patch of weeds. They're tall enough to hide us while we crouch and face each other.

"Let go of me," she says.

I release her arm—that old, familiar fear of overstepping a girl's boundaries. And yet, out here, a guy in my situation could be way worse. She doesn't seem to get that.

"How can you trust me this much?" I ask her. "We barely know each other. I could be dangerous."

"If that was true, you wouldn't be telling me this."

I frown at her. "You trusted me before I said it, though."

"I can tell you're not like that, Kip. You're a collector, not a raider."

"A what?"

"A collector. You go out on supply runs and—"

"Okay, I get it. I'm a collector. But I'm also heavily armed, and I haven't seen a girl in three years."

She seems taken aback by this. "Oh."

I'm about to explain when she cuts me off.

"Well, I haven't seen a guy in over two years since my neighbor Artie left his house and never came back. So I'm in the same boat. What difference does it make?"

Now I'm flat-out suspicious. I'm a guy carrying knives

and guns telling this isolated young woman I might be a rapist, and she's either too dumb to realize it, or she's playing games with me.

"Tell me you're not this naïve," I say in a harsh whisper, "because *I'm* definitely not. If you're not the least bit scared of me, then either you're too stupid to be out here—no offense—or you're leading me into a trap. How do I know *that* station"—I point at the Lubroline—"isn't hiding three guys with shotguns who are going to—"

"Go screw yourself," she throws back at me. "I just saved your life."

"And I'm grateful for that, Melanie. Really, I am. But my dad is going to die in less than two days if I don't get him the antibiotics in my pack. So it was nice meeting you, and I hope I didn't offend you, but I have to go."

"You're just going to feed him pills, huh? How do you know you have the right ones? Are they broad or narrow-spectrum?"

I'm not surprised she knows this stuff. It's Survivalism 101.

"One of each," I say, maybe a little too smugly. "Nafcillin and Vancomycin."

"And what are your dad's symptoms?"

"He has sepsis."

"Okay, but what did he look like when you left the house?"

I describe all of the important details, down to his heart rate and the way he was breathing. She nods along with my words and never rushes me. I notice she has coppery green eyes and a light dusting of freckles visible beneath the layer of grime on her cheeks.

"Cold and clammy skin," she says, repeating my description, "dizziness when you tried to move him to the couch, a rapid heart rate, breathing rate—I'd say he's on the verge of septic shock."

"What are you, a doctor?"

"No, but my Mom's a nurse. *Was*, I mean. I live with her and my sister."

"What about your dad?"

Her expression hardens, and her eyes take on a distant look.

"He couldn't handle it. All this, I mean."

She drops her gaze like she's ashamed.

"It wasn't your fault, Melanie. I'm sorry you had to go through that."

"It's okay."

She flashes me a look of revelation, as if she has just remembered something.

"Your father needs medicine, but not pills."

"Huh?" I say stupidly.

"You need to inject the medicine directly into his blood steam, intravenously, and he's going to need fluids, too. Otherwise, his blood pressure will drop, and he'll go into septic shock. Then his organs will start to fail—"

"Oh God," I say, awash suddenly in self-loathing. "You're right."

How could I have been so stupid?

"Kip," she says, "look at me."

When I do, all I see is urgency, and not a trace of pity.

"I can give you what you need to save him," Melanie says.

"You have an I.V. set-up?"

She nods. "The one at my house is broken. I wanted to replace it. But you need it more than I do—and besides, I won't be able to get home until I fix my bike anyway. That's more important."

"What does your bike need?"

"A new chain."

"You rode a bike out here without a spare chain?"

"You know what?" she says, scowling at me. "That's right. I did. Sort of like how you forgot what sepsis was and how to treat it."

I sigh impatiently and look away at nothing but a soft wall of smelly, bug-infested weeds. Our coveralls are probably covered in ticks right now. Not that I care the slightest bit about ticks.

"Let's go somewhere safe," I tell her. "Then we'll talk about this."

I lead the way, feeling like a jerk. But Melanie is right, which makes bumping into her one of the luckiest breaks I've had so far.

The Lubroline station is one of those quick-serve, oil-changing facilities where you drive through one side and out the other ten minutes later. A small building made of brick and glass, it looks like the last place a rational person —especially a trained survivalist—would use as shelter. All six of its garage doors are busted, and the floor is covered in a broad carpet of broken glass.

"It's so I can hear if someone's up here," Melanie says. "Follow my steps."

Up here?

I place my boots in the clean spots on the floor where Melanie has cleverly made a winding trail.

There's a row of panels built into the concrete floor, which I imagine the technicians once slid open to access the car's undercarriage. A raider with a crowbar and enough time on his hands could probably crack one of these open without much difficulty and find the space below, which I'm sure is where she's been hiding.

"Those are sealed," Melanie says, thrusting her chin to indicate the nearest one.

"Good," I say. "I was going to ask."

She whirls on me, gracefully avoiding the glass shards. Maybe she was a ballerina once.

"Do you think all girls are stupid," she says, "or just me?"

I lift my hands and motion for her to slow down. "All I said was—"

"I don't care what you said. It's in your tone, your body language. I saved your life, and the only thanks I get is accusations that I'm leading you into a trap, or subtle remarks meant to make me feel stupid."

Her voice reverberates inside the building.

"Keep your voice down," I whisper.

"See? There you go again," she says, lowering it only slightly. "I *know* that."

I feel like gritting my teeth. She's going to get us killed.

"Fine," I say in a grating whisper, "go ahead and scream at me. It's obvious you want an audience. How about a horde of infected? Will that do it for you?"

She looks away, cheeks rippling as she clenches her teeth. The first girl I've seen in three years, and she totally hates me.

"Do you want my help or not?" she asks me in a quiet, stern voice.

"What I want is that I.V. setup so I can save my father's life. You want to trade for a bike chain, that's fine. You're lucky I don't plan on just taking it from you."

Her next motions are so swift that I don't comprehend what she's doing until an arrow with a sharp metal tip is staring me in the face, tightly drawn against the bowstring.

It took her two seconds, tops, to ready the weapon. Her boots never even crunched the glass.

Mine definitely make a crunching sound as I take a cautious step back, arms flying up to defend my face.

"What is your fucking problem?" she says.

"*Melanie.* Will you just relax?"

The arrowhead is a well-crafted point of glistening steel with ridges along the blades meant to give it teeth. The way she yanked it out of her quiver and nocked it—I didn't even know that was possible, except in the movies.

Maybe she's killed guys like me before. Why not? It obvious this isn't her first time out here, which is more than I can say for myself.

She needs my help, though. There's no denying that.

"I know you won't shoot me, Melanie," I say. "That's not what I'm afraid of."

"Then why are you being like this? What *are* you afraid of?"

Her bow is trembling now, the arrow still nocked against a string, bent at an angle that could end my life. Faced with the possibility of dying, though I don't fear it at all, I tell her a truth I'm just beginning to understand.

"I'm afraid of what you might mean to me when this is over."

6

I've always excelled at embarrassing myself around women.

Flirting with them at parties, working with them in study groups, even chatting with them online were all just opportunities for me to screw up.

Even female teachers at school were a struggle. Peltham Park High had a few attractive ones, and I was always such a mumbling kiss-ass around them that a couple of jocks once started a rumor about how they had caught me taking pictures of my English Lit teacher, Mrs. Russell, during class. (It wasn't true. My cellphone didn't even have a camera.) Nothing ever came of it except a few jokes, but for the rest of that year, I never took out my cellphone in any class taught by a woman.

The worst was when I had sketched, then framed a portrait of Hailey Bushnell—my girlfriend during the last four months of sophomore year—and given it to her as a birthday gift along with a bouquet of roses. We continued dating for the next three weeks, but she never mentioned it until she broke up with me at the start of summer. In her words, the drawing was an example of how "intense" I was about our relationship. She said it made her notice "little things" about me, like how I always looked in her eyes after kissing her, like I was "counting our unborn children."

For the next few weeks, I stayed indoors and brooded about it, until I found out from a mutual friend that Hailey had been planning for months to spend the summer in North Carolina at her aunt's beach house. (The woman also had a place in Italy, where she "summered.") I called up Hailey's online profile and discovered—it wasn't even July 4th yet—that she had already found herself a tanned, muscular, lifeguard boyfriend.

Still, I vowed never to sketch a portrait of a girl ever again. I was damned good at it, too. I also vowed never to tell a girlfriend how much I cared about her until she made the plunge first. The Outbreak made both of those promises unnecessary, but I'm sure I would have followed through with them. That's how insecure I was back then.

Turns out I haven't changed a bit.

As I stand here staring at that shivering arrowhead aimed at my neck, deadly weapons strapped all over my body to protect against the endless threat of murderers, mindless cannibals, and a killer virus—all three of which live, literally, in my neighborhood—the only fear that goes through my mind is one that can be summed up in seven simple words.

Now she isn't going to like me.

"I'm sorry," I say. "I don't mean to be intense"—damn it, Hailey—"but it's just that..."

"It's okay," Melanie says, lowering the bow. She tips her head in the direction she wants me to follow. "Come on. I'll show you the way in."

She stabs the arrow back into its quiver and slips the

bow over one shoulder, so the string lies diagonally across her chest. We make our way carefully over the broken glass until we reach an unmarked metal door with a simple chain-and-padlock setup.

"Is this the only lock?"

She takes out a small key, pops it open, and frees the chain. Quietly, she slips it out, link by link, then lays it on the floor next to the doorframe.

"Take out your flashlight," she says.

I dig it out. Melanie opens the door, and I flash the beam into the darkness to reveal a bending, concrete stairway that leads downstairs.

"What about it?" I say.

She gently takes my flashlight and shines it on the edge of the first step. I see a thread-like glimmer running parallel to the floor. At first, I think it's a strand from an unfinished spider web, but a closer look tells me it's actually a thread someone has placed there.

"No way," I say in amazement. "A trip line?"

"I always thought it was called a trigger line," she says.

"What is it connected to?"

"A hand grenade."

"I have to see this. Is that the only line?"

I'm already grabbing the flashlight from her hands.

"Yes. But Kip, be careful."

I step into the stairwell and shine the beam down the angular tunnel between the handrails. Craning my neck, I catch sight of a small, greenish globe hanging there that must be the grenade.

"Nice work," I say. "This is next-level stuff."

Glancing over my shoulder, I catch a smile Melanie quickly hides, like she's embarrassed by her own pride.

"Maybe now you won't think I'm such a noob," she says.

I haven't heard that word in years, and it sends a warm wave of nostalgia over me. Once I'm out of the stairwell, Melanie closes the door and locks it back up.

"So how do you get down there?" I ask her. "Without losing a leg, I mean."

"It's this way."

I feel like a dumb puppy following its owner around in hopes it'll get a treat. I don't mind. I'm learning. This is way better than the trash heap I probably would have built for myself as a semi-permanent shelter.

Igniting her own flashlight, Melanie guides me away from the rigged stairwell and through a short hallway in back that leads to a tiny, one-man office. The place smells like decay and contains nothing of value, only a cracked and pitted wraparound desk made of particleboard.

She falls into a crouch, flashlight beam illuminating a human skeleton beneath the desk.

I pull back at the sight of it. I've never been this close to a dead body, though to call this a body is a stretch. The grinning skeleton is mostly intact and lies stretched across a torn canvas blanket, making it look as though the person was asleep at time of death.

Melanie pulls the blanket—and the bones along with it—away from its original spot. In the beam of her flashlight, I see a thin board about three feet long and a foot and a half wide on the floor, pushed up against the wall. It lies there as if to cover something beneath it.

Melanie lifts the board and reveals something even more impressive than the grenade trap in the stairwell: a hole someone has dug through the concrete.

It's a tunnel leading underground.

"No way," I say, mixing the words with a chuckle. "You have got to be kidding me."

She arranges the set-up so she can pull it back over the hole from inside. I like the way she thinks. She and my father would get along famously, and I'm struck with the sudden urge to introduce them to each other.

"Go ahead," she tells me.

Without even a thought that this might be a trap, I go first, dropping several feet to yet another concrete floor. I ignite my flashlight and watch Melanie wriggle through. I catch her as she drops.

Suddenly she's in my arms, her face a few inches from mine, breath warm against my chin. Our utility belts are bulky and press into each other, making it awkward to stand that close, but I barely notice it. For the next two seconds, I feel more comfortable than I've ever felt with another person, especially a girl.

She pats my arm impatiently and thrusts her chin at the darkness behind me. Terrified, I swing around, pulling the Glock out of my chest holster to aim at what I'm certain is someone sneaking up on us. But all I see is an empty room.

Well, not exactly *empty*. The room is full of supplies. I set down my pack and approach the piles lying all over the floor, growing more amazed with each passing second.

There's very little of what my father calls "bulk valuables" down here, items like gasoline, medicine, water, food, and ammo that are prized in large amounts. But there's a whole lot of what he calls "godly trinkets." These are items that possess high value on a purely individual level, like a topographical map, a compass, lock picks, or a functioning rifle.

With the exception of guns, I see all of those items and more. They've been gathered into small, unorganized piles scattered throughout the room, as if the person who brought them down here was hoarding treasure with no end goal in mind.

"The I.V. stuff is in that garbage bag against the wall," Melanie tells me, pointing.

"Thanks. I'll get it after I help you find that chain."

"Just take it. I trust you."

I kneel in front of the garbage bag and dig through it. The bags and tubes are still in their original seals, though of course, I'm still going to disinfect the hell out of them when I get back, just in case. I leave the bottles of saline solution behind. Too much weight. Plus, I can make that stuff from scratch back home.

With the extra gear, my pack is now several pounds heavier than it was this morning. Hopefully it won't slow me down. I lay it against the wall and turn to Melanie.

"Did you scavenge all this stuff?" I ask her, throwing the beam of light at her as she moves across the room. She stops at a metal table and lights a candle next to a box full of them —yet another precious item, a luxury to some.

"My father found this place during a supply run," she says absently. "He made a map for us—my mother and my little sister and me—in case we ever had to leave the house. It's more of a temporary shelter. You couldn't live down here."

"No, probably not," I say.

She suggested earlier that her father took his own life, a terrible thing I can't imagine having to live with. I keep my mouth shut so as not to remind her of it. But I'm curious as to why a man with a wife and two daughters, who was brave enough to go out on supply runs, would abandon his family like that.

She lights a few more candles, creating a warm glow that reminds me of my father sprawled across the couch in front of the blazing hearth in our living room. I click off the flashlight, slip it into my pocket, and approach her. She turns to me. The candlelight shivers along one side of her face, exposing an eye agleam with moisture.

"He left us," she said.

"What do you mean?"

A tear breaks away and runs down her cheek. "More than a year ago. The sun was coming up. I never woke up early, but that day I did. I don't know why I looked outside. My window was boarded up, but I looked through the crack into our backyard, and I saw him."

"What was he doing?"

I place my hands on her elbows and feel the way she's shivering, not from cold but from the memory of whatever it is she saw her father do.

"He was carrying his pack and a laundry bag full of stuff. It was food. He took some of our food and left, and I watched him run to a van that was waiting at the other end of our yard. When the door opened, I saw people inside. Men and women with bags of stuff. He got in and sat down on the floor. He didn't even look at our house, Kip. Not once. He just kept his eyes on the floor. Then a man stuck his head out and looked around. He closed the door really slowly, like he didn't want to wake us up. And then they left."

A list of possible explanations runs through my mind, but only one makes any sense at all.

"Melanie, what did your father do before the Outbreak?"

She blinks at me. "He was a doctor. A surgeon."

"Jesus, I'm sorry."

She nods. I don't have to explain it to her. She already knows.

A surgeon. I've heard of this sort of thing before—

people with valuable skills being recruited by bands of survivors hoping to create their own isolated communities, usually up in the mountains where the infected, raiders, and, to a lesser degree, slavers, aren't as likely to travel.

If it was a man being recruited, like Melanie's father, the leader of the community might promise to set him up with a beautiful young wife. Maybe even two or three. Any sort of doctor would be a godsend in a community like that. Her miserable prick of a father was probably waking up right now to a pair of teenage wives asleep on either side of him.

"Was he the one who taught you how to use that bow and set up those traps?" I ask her.

She shakes her head, looking down at the floor.

"I taught myself," she says. "I practiced every day after he left. We were running out of food. I knew I'd have to go out on a supply run someday, but I never expected it to be like this, Kip. Not this bad."

She turns away from me, sniffles, and wipes her eyes dry.

"Melanie, how long have you been out here?"

"Almost two weeks. Oh God, Kip, I need to go home. I need to see my mom and my sister. They're probably freaking out. Sarah's only twelve. She has nightmares that make her scream at night. I can't imagine..."

Her voice trails off as she shakes her head at the thought.

"You could hike back to them, couldn't you?" I ask her.

She gives me an incredulous look. "Without a gun? Are you crazy? And I only have twenty-two arrows left. What if that's not enough?"

I nod. "I see what you mean. Where's the bicycle?"

"It's hidden in the trees, beneath a tarp with a dead viral on it."

Viral. That's one I haven't heard in a while.

"All this stuff," she says in a voice thick with rage, "and not a single *fucking* bicycle chain. I've looked through all of it. Every single bag and box. But the one thing I need isn't here."

"It's okay," I tell her. "We'll get that chain. But first, we need to figure out where to look."

An idea hits me, accompanied by a memory of looking into a building and seeing what looked to be chains scattered across the floor. It's so obvious I can't believe I didn't think of it sooner.

"They don't sell them at SuperMarts," I tell her. "But that's okay. I know a place."

"Where?"

I smile at her. "Ever heard of Tommy's Bike Shack?"

7

We're about two miles away from Tommy's when our empty stomachs just can't hold out any longer.

Melanie and I talk about our old lives as we break out PowerBars, powdered milk and sugar that we mix with water, and tinned peaches and pears. It's a good meal, and I hide my burp afterward.

"Don't," Melanie says.

"What?"

"Hide it. It doesn't bother me."

A low burp grumbles out of her throat. I respond with one of my own. We smile at each other, though my smile quickly fades away. This won't last. The more I enjoy her company, the more painful it'll be when we have to say good-bye.

We pack our garbage so as not to leave a trail, then make our way behind the buildings along Route 1 toward the bike shop.

"Did you ever date anyone at school?" she asks me. "I mean, other than Hailey."

I slow down, almost stopping completely. "You know about that?"

"Everyone did. She slept with, like, five guys that summer."

"I don't want to know."

"So," she says, "was there anyone else?"

"Why do you care?" My tone is playful, but I'm curious.

"Geez, Kip. I'm just making conversation."

We make our way through thick underbrush in silence. Thorns snag my coverall. It's a crappy path, but safer than using the road or crossing the lots.

I can't stand the silence and wish she would keep talking. But Melanie wants an answer. She's even pouting.

"There was this one girl," I say. "Nancy Kim."

"Ninja Nancy?" she says in utter shock.

I'm even more appalled.

"She was Korean," I say. "Ninjas are Chinese. I can't believe you of all people would call her that."

"*Everyone* called her that. Did you live under a rock or something? Nancy used to climb all over the buildings. She almost got suspended one time for scaling the atrium. You mean to tell me you two dated and you never knew about this?"

Of course I knew about Nancy's weird climbing addiction. It was the reason I broke up with her after only three weeks of "officially" dating. She spent every weekend out with her climbing buddies scaling granite cliff sides, something my fear of heights never allowed me to do. We had zero chemistry.

"We didn't go out very long," I say.

"You know she kicked a boy in the nuts once?"

A long howl takes us by surprise. It sounds human—though whether it's a man, woman, or child, I can't tell. It's coming from inside the outlet mall we happen to be passing by, the one I considered making shelter in the evening before.

"Hide over here," I say, pulling her to a Dumpster.

We crouch behind it and wait.

The high-pitched howling begins again. It's the sound of a person in pain. I take out the Glock. Melanie already has an arrow nocked against her bow.

"Sounds like a fox or a wounded dog," she says.

"You think?" I can't get the image of a wounded old lady out of my head. "I thought it sounded more like a person."

"Definitely not infected," she says.

"Definitely not."

We both know infected don't howl. They don't scream, either. They huff and hiss and growl, but that's about it. I'm still not sure why that is.

We listen for a third howl. The first two were definitely coming from inside the building in front of us, which stands about a dozen feet away from the tree line. But all we hear now is wind tussling the tree leaves.

It comes a third time—long and pitiful.

Above us, in a window without glass, an old man suddenly appears. He's shirtless, his hair and beard long, scraggly, and gray-yellow from malnourishment. He's definitely infected—I can tell by the red-veined eyes, the unnaturally pale skin—but he's in the early stages, probably not too far gone to speak. Like my mother when we first locked her in the bedroom.

At this stage, an infected person is still considered to be a viable meal for other, more infected individuals. This old man should have been eaten a long time ago.

"What is he doing?" Melanie says.

I watch as the old man sticks his head and his bony

white shoulders through the window. He looks around until he sees us, then his eyes go wide. I can't tell if he's afraid or relieved to see a non-infected person.

He speaks to us, and when he does, his voice sounds like the howl from before.

"You kids need to runnn... Runnnnn away."

I want to stand beneath the window and talk to the man, find out what happened, how he has managed to survive this long. But before I can do anything, the man reaches back, grabs something, and sticks it out the window. It's a canvas bag attached to a rope. Small, about the size of a human head. He lowers it with jerking movements.

"He's giving it to us," I say.

"What is it?"

"I don't know. I'll grab it."

I drop my pack and crouch-walk over to the building to receive the canvas bag. It's light, airy, filled with what at first feels like twigs, or maybe hay.

I don't have much time to identify it. The old man releases a moan and slips through the window. He falls toward me. I drop the bag and extend my arms. It's only a two-story drop, but the man is old. I forget he's infected as I catch him and fall back, cushioning his fall with my entire body.

"Kip," Melanie says, running to me.

She does the considerate thing and rolls him off of me before he can touch my face or neck. I scramble back and stare at him, at the long sores covering his back, the bruises everywhere. He's shivering now and howling like before.

Melanie grabs the canvas bag and steps away.

I look at the old man. "What about—"

"He's infected," she says. "Nothing we can do. Let's go."

"But—"

"Kip, let's go!"

I follow her away from the old man. He'll attract every infected in a mile radius with the noise he's making. Already I can hear them shuffling toward the back of the outlet mall from the parking lot in front.

"Jesus," I say without breath. "Jesus Christ."

"Shh..."

Behind us, the infected make choking, ripping, and gagging noises as they tear the old man apart. I look back only once to see a group of them hunched in a circle around him, biting and tearing and slurping. It reminds me of the guy who had been tossed out of the Jeep earlier.

I resolve to get back home as soon as possible, and never to leave my house again.

We hide next to a broken-down ATM machine behind a bank, one of those outdoor ones with the overhanging roof to protect customers from rain as they make their transactions. A different bank from the one I stopped at the day before, though I don't see any signs with a name for this one.

"Let's see what's inside," Melanie says, passing me the canvas bag.

"What? You don't want to do it?"

She shakes her head. "He gave it to you."

"He gave it to both of us."

I open the bag anyway and look inside.

"Holy crap," I say. "You've gotta be kidding."

"What is it?" She cranes her neck to peer inside.

We're both stunned, and a little confused, at the discovery. It's not twigs or hay, which is how it had felt earlier, but fireworks. Specifically, fire*crackers*, the ones that are strung together and sound like a machine gun when they go off.

But why would anyone have fireworks in a place

where a single gunshot is enough to attract a horde of flesh-eating maniacs? Anyone dumb enough to set off even a handful of these things would be instantly surrounded.

"What do you think they're for?" Melanie says.

"I don't know. I guess we can't ask the old man anymore, can we?"

She frowns. "You know, you could say thank you. He was infected. If he had touched you—"

"I know," I say. "I know. Thank you. But we need to hurry. We have to get to that bicycle shop before dark."

"I agree. But promise me one thing, Kip."

"I'm listening."

"We're in this together. So let's make decisions together. Going after that old man was risky, and I don't plan on dying because you want to be a hero."

"I wasn't trying to be a hero."

"Okay, so you were curious about the bag. What if it had been a trap? Like a grenade or something?"

"Who would lower a live grenade? You'd call every infected person in the county with a stunt like that."

"I'm just saying!"

"Hey." I place a hand on her arm. "I promise. We'll decide things together from now on."

She gives me a hard look—still a wall between us—and follows it with a nod. I wave her in the direction of the bike shop.

"Let's go."

"Wait."

She grabs my pack and yanks me around to face her.

"What's wrong?" I say.

"Nothing." She gives me a somber look. "It's just that—you're a good man, Kip. Your dad must be proud."

"He *is* proud," I say, "but he won't be for much longer if I don't help him."

She nods to show she understands. I stuff the firecrackers into my pack and head toward our destination.

Though the bicycle shop has obviously been ransacked, the front door is closed.

That's my first indication that something is off. In most ransacked buildings, the doors are wide open, either because the looter left it that way, confident that he had scavenged everything of value, or because the infected have barged their way inside. Normally, with the doors closed, I wouldn't be able to tell if the place has already been hit, but it's pretty obvious here considering how badly the windows have been smashed, and all the useless debris littering the parking lot that could only have come from inside. Among the debris are bicycle helmets in bright colors for young girls, little round reflectors, cycling shorts, and a brass bell.

But no chains. Those are hopefully still inside.

"Why do you think the doors are closed?" Melanie says.

I smile. "We're on the same wavelength. I was wondering the same thing."

"Yeah, right," she says.

"I *was*."

"Okay. Then what's your theory?"

I lift my eyebrows as if to say, *Isn't it obvious?*

"Someone's inside," I tell her, taking out my gun and checking it. "But not raiders, since I don't see a getaway vehicle. And it's not a looter since obviously the place has already been cleaned out. My guess is someone is hiding out in there. Maybe the person's wounded."

Melanie gives a ponderous nod, as if to admit she hadn't considered this.

"That's what I was thinking, too," she says.

"Yeah, right."

She grins at me, then casts her eyes down at the gun.

"That'll be too noisy," she says. "If it's a survivor, we won't need weapons."

"Unless it's a trap," I say.

We agree to go in with weapons bared, though not with the express intention of using them unless the shit really hits the fan. Melanie offers to take the lead. I resist, but her logic makes sense. She's wielding a compound bow, which is a silent weapon. If someone does leap out of the shadows to attack us, her bow will take them out without alerting the infected.

We make our move, quietly opening the front door, which is unlocked. Melanie and I look at each other. We're thinking the same thing. If the door isn't locked or boarded up, then maybe no one is in here after all. Nevertheless, we make our way inside with caution.

The interior is dark except where the afternoon light spills in through the broken windows. I see scattered magazine pages, receipts, and other trash in the bright patches. I shine my flashlight on the walls. The bikes are all gone—no surprise there. I pass the beam all over the floor, checking for footprints, but the dust looked undisturbed.

"They should be around here," I say. "Let's head to the back. I looked in through those windows on my way by here yesterday and saw what looked like chains."

I press the business end of the flashlight to my belly, in case the light gives away our position to someone lurking in the shadows with a gun. We stick to the walls to make ourselves harder to see. Part of me thinks we're overdoing it a bit. The dust on the floor shows no sign at all that someone has been here recently.

As we creep along the walls to the back, I imagine shiny

new bikes propped up in rows all over the place, wheels hanging on the walls, and parents strolling with their children, thinking of summer bike rides they'll take together. It had been such an innocent place once. A safe place. Tommy Poretti, the owner, had been one of the happiest people I'd ever known. I remember his booming voice, his thick Boston accent, and his love of bicycles, despite his stocky Italian frame.

Kip Garrity, his voice belted out in my memory of him. *Been watching them Sox? Hey, tell the old Marine I said hi.*

He and my father were old friends. Tommy called my dad a Marine to piss him off. My father returned the gesture by telling Tommy to start stocking motorcycles like a real man.

Moisture has risen in my eyes.

"What's wrong?" Melanie says.

I turn, blinking it away, glad it's not tears. What kind of a wimp cries about two old men trading insults in a bike shop?

"It's nothing." I shake my head.

"You used to come here a lot."

Now I nod, though I do so grudgingly to discourage her from going deeper. I have to remind myself that Melanie has lost just as much as I have. No reason for me to call so much attention to my own sadness.

She sees that I'm uncomfortable and makes her way toward the back area, where the repair guys had once been stationed. Telling myself to get a grip, I follow her.

We search for a few moments until Melanie speaks in an excited whisper that is still dangerously loud.

"There they are!"

She covers her mouth, looking alarmed at her own carelessness, then points happily at the chains.

"That's them," I say.

She lifts a pair of chains, blows dust off of them, and inspects them as if they were diamond necklaces.

"Perfect," she says before swinging off her backpack to stuff them inside. "Why do you think the looters left them? Ooh, I wonder if there's a can of oil around here." She gets up and starts looking around. "I wish there was a bike here for you, Kip. But you seem like more of a motorcycle guy. Of course, that would be way too loud."

I'm about to agree with her but stop at the sound of a ragged moan. It's coming from outside—so close that I'm surprised there isn't a rotting head in the window.

Melanie and I drop to our bellies and crawl away from the patches of light on the floor that threaten to expose us. From our hiding spot around a corner, I slip the clamshell mirror out of my belt, pry it open with my thumb, and lift it to get a view of the windows. The moans haven't stopped. Now I hear a whole chorus of them.

Through the empty square, I see only the gray-white of sky. Rising into a standing position gives me a better vantage point, and I gradually see rooftops and a streetlamp, walls and busted windows, followed by human heads and shoulders. A throng of infected, marching up Route 1. The closest ones are only a dozen yards away.

I stuff the mirror into my pocket and motion for Melanie to follow me. We're on our way to the exit when a noise makes us freeze—the *scrape scrape* of feet dragging themselves over dead leaves. It's coming from the window by the *back* door, not the front.

"We're surrounded," I whisper.

Right now, the infected seem to be parting around Tommy's Bike Shack like river water around a jutting stone.

We need to be careful. A single noise loud enough to attract one or two could lead to an entire horde.

I look for cover, but there is literally nothing inside the former store to hide us from the windows.

For once, I am at a complete loss. I'm just plain scared. I hate the feeling of being surrounded. Once, when I was thirteen, a group of kids surrounded me in enemy territory during a game of Capture the Flag. Instead of running or giving up, I started throwing punches.

"I've got an idea," Melanie says.

The panic recedes. I look at her face in the shadows, and I see a smile. Goddamn, she's tough.

"What is it?"

I'm nearly floored by her next words.

"Pass me those firecrackers," she says.

It doesn't take us long to get set up.

"I'll count to three," I tell Melanie, who nods behind the raised compact bow. "Then I'll light it."

Imagine her crouching there and facing the window. One leg is folded beneath her weight, the other extended for balance, her right elbow pulled back to keep the bowstring tight. She looks like an Amazon girl-warrior in modern-day clothing.

One thing about this picture is strikingly odd, and that is the strip of mottled, red-and-white firecrackers hanging from the arrow.

Now, imagine me holding a matchbook, about to strike the flame that will ignite the fuse uniting all of these mini-explosions.

Before this happens, I'll explain what is at risk. The shot needs to be perfect. High enough so the window's ledge doesn't tear off the fireworks, but not so high that the arrow hits the top part of the frame and sticks there. I'm not worried about the sides—it's a broad window, and I know Melanie is good at this.

However, one shot is all she gets. If she messes it up, the fireworks will remain inside the building. They'll go off, and every infected in the entire man-made world will close around Tommy's Bike Shack to rip open our bellies and devour our internal organs while we die slowly from blood loss.

"One," I say, staring at Melanie's unblinking green eyes.

God, she's beautiful. Even with the dirt on her face. For some reason, I see this as a good moment to tell her that.

"You're gorgeous," I tell her.

A corner of her mouth rises—a desperate smile that floods me with warmth.

"Was that two?" she says.

The explosive strip hangs perfectly still, Melanie's poise steady.

"No. This is." I strike a match. "Two."

I bring the match toward the fuse, which splits into a web work that will light each cracker in quick succession. A strip this length will pop for a full minute, maybe more, assuming the moisture that has mottled its red-and-white stripes has left it dry enough to pop at all.

"Three."

I fire up the main fuse. Immediately, the bowstring snaps and the arrow disappears. The bow barely flinches. The shot is a clean one.

She did it.

From the trees behind Tommy's Bike Shack, the firecrackers emit a crackling noise that sends chills through my entire body. Melanie and I grab our packs and bolt through the back door, into the trees, where we immediately make a beeline southward, away from the noise.

As we run, we throw glances over our shoulders to make sure we aren't being followed. The firecrackers are still popping like mad. Luckily the river of infected was coming from the north, which means our path southward is mostly clear.

We have to cross Route 1 to get back to the Lubroline station and Melanie's bicycle hidden beneath the tarp ("with a dead viral on it," as she had put it). Now that the firecrackers have probably alerted every infected person within a mile range, we need to make sure we don't call attention while doing it.

We skulk on a leaf-covered driveway between a shady motel and a seafood shack. The driveway empties into Route 1, on which more infected have gathered like rioters. Dozens of them head north, hobbling in their eagerness to reach the fireworks, which are almost dead. A couple more go off, and then that's it.

"We should fire another one," Melanie says.

"There's one more strip," I say. "You ready?"

She nods and reaches for another arrow as I go for the canvas bag in my pack.

Behind us, a man's voice says, "Don't move or I'll blow your fucking heads off."

8

"Toss the weapons over here," the man says, "then turn toward me real slow, like molasses."

Melanie and I are still crouched against the building, facing Route 1, too alarmed to do anything but stare into each other's wide, frightened eyes. She's holding her bow in one hand, the other halfway to her quiver. My fingers are on my holstered Glock. Soon, the infected will lose track of where the fireworks came from and start fanning out, and everyone—including the man behind us—will be in a world of trouble.

"I said toss your weapons and come toward me. Now."

Melanie and I do as we're told. Without my pistol, I feel like I'm missing a hand. We turn around, press our backs to the wall, and lift our arms in surrender.

The area behind the motel is a strip of parking spaces. The Jeep I saw at the Citizens' Bank is parked sideways across three of them, facing us. My stomach sinks at the sight of it, especially when I recognize the man with the neck tattoo staring at us from the back seat.

The one who spoke to us wears the same faded red

bandanna and holds the same automatic rifle as yesterday. Instead of standing in the front passenger seat of the vehicle like before, he's in a shooting stance a few feet away. The rifle is an M16—serious firepower even in a situation like this. You'd have to be insane to bring a weapon like that out here.

Unless you're hunting something that might shoot back.

"What do you want?" I ask the tattooed man in the Jeep, since I know he's the leader.

He doesn't respond. He just stares at me. His eyes are wide, like he's watching a lottery in which one more lucky number stands between him and a big win.

Bandanna approaches me, flips the rifle around, and jabs the butt stock into my stomach. I double over, the breath knocked out of me.

Melanie places a hand on my shoulder. I brush it off and rise, quietly struggling to breathe. Bandanna steps back and aims the rifle's deadly barrel at me again.

"Your stash," he says.

It's hard to concentrate while staring down the barrel of a gun that could tear you to pieces. I blink at him, frozen with indecision. *My* stash is back on Exeter Road, but Melanie's stash is in the Lubroline station down the street. I'm not sure what he's talking about.

"I don't mean the girl's stash, either," the man says as if he's read my mind. He pulls his lips back in a grisly smile that reveals a twisted mess of brown and yellow teeth. "I know that one probably ain't shit. Yeah, we'll get to it later, but what I want to know is where *you* come from, kid. You ain't from this part of town, are ya? You got new gear, a fancy pack, a nice Glock. I *know* there's more where that came from."

I glance at my pistol, which he has kicked back toward

the Jeep. No one has moved to pick it up. The driver of the vehicle, who still looks like a wild man from the mountains, stares intently at Melanie. The one with the tattoo hasn't moved or changed his expression at all.

They won't wait much longer for me to answer. There's no way I'll give them my address. Then I think: what if they threaten Melanie?

"*Caballeros*," the guy with the neck tattoo says in a surprisingly crisp and springy voice. "Let's finish this at base camp, shall we?"

Caballeros. That's Spanish for "gentlemen," only there isn't anything Spanish about him. He's just having fun. To them, this is probably another day at the office.

I barely have a chance to blink as the guy with the M16 rushes forward. He jabs the rifle's butt stock into my face, knocking me out.

9

"Wake up, little scavenger."

He says it in a sing-song voice that reminds me of the lullaby that begins with, "Hush, little baby." Behind my closed and heavy eyelids, I picture the way my mother looked when I saw her crouched in her bedroom, only the keyhole between us, her face covered in slash marks.

I don't want to go there ever again. I open my eyes with a gasp.

The first thing I notice is the dark ceiling high above me, followed by the way the cold, stagnant air smells, a combination of concrete and gasoline. My right eye remains half shut, sealed by what I know is dried blood. It coats my face like a layer of hardened paint.

Something floats into my field of vision and stops dead center.

My lucky rabbit's foot.

"Guess these blasted things don't really work, huh?" the man holding it says before flinging it away into the darkness.

He bends over me until all I see is his repulsive, familiar face, the black rose tattoo staining his fleshy neck. He's chewing something with a noisy smacking sound. It smells like peanut butter PowerBar.

"You know, these are quite delectable," he says with a few more smacks. He holds up the half-eaten bar still in its wrapper. "I haven't enjoyed one in quite some time."

He takes a huge bite out of it, then tosses the rest away and wipes his hand against his T-shirt.

The guy is uglier than I remember, his dark eyes embedded in a nest of dirty wrinkles, his black beard like tightly packed pubic hair, sprinkled with grime. As he grins down at me, I notice in the thin yellow light of a nearby bulb or lantern that his teeth are slick with PowerBar he is too lazy to lick away.

I lift my head to glance at my surroundings, despite my fear that he might hit me for moving. But he doesn't. Instead, he pulls back and watches me. I see his two buddies in different positions around the long wooden table to which my arms and legs are tied with rope. The skinny, wild-looking driver of the Jeep sits on a wooden crate, while the other stands by a table on which various metal instruments have been laid out.

Torture devices? Or just tools for fixing the place?

My head and neck hurt too much to lift any further. Quick glances to my left and right tell me we're in a dark warehouse full of steel-beam shelves, each a dozen feet tall, and mostly empty. The only light comes one of the shelves to my left, where a gas lantern lets off a weak glow that reminds me of a campfire in a dark forest at night—a place I'd much rather be than here.

Melanie.

What have they done with her?

"Please," I say.

"You're shivering," the tattooed man says before throwing an amused glance at the others. "He's shivering. After everything that's happened, all it takes is three bottom-feeders like us to scare the piss out of him."

"Please," I say again. "Where is she?"

The black-rose-and-barbed-wire tattoo stretches as the man crosses his arms and looks at me askance.

"Hey now, how about you let me lead this inquisition?" he says.

I hate how familiar his voice is, and how harmless I once found it. A sharp pain grows in my head from resting it on the flat wooden surface.

"You look familiar," he says. "Tell me: where have I glimpsed your youthful visage?"

I don't answer. He shows me the hairy back of his right hand.

"I asked you a question, young squire."

Fuck. Being hit again will sap more of my strength. I have to keep him talking long enough to figure out an alternative.

"The Exxon station," I say. "You—you were the cash register guy—"

"And you're talking out your ass," he says in a single breath, chuckling lightly at the end of it.

I've made him uncomfortable. Good. Fuck him.

Bandanna interrupts. "I thought you said you were an FBI ag—"

"Shut your unclean mouth, you rag-headed faggot."

Bandanna makes a *tsk* sound and goes back to whatever he was doing.

Despite the broken glass in my skull—that's how it feels, anyway—I lift my head to glance at them again. Bandanna is now sharpening a hunting knife against a whetstone. The skinny, wild one is still sitting on the crate, probably staring at me, though I can't tell since his long, wavy hair blocks his face from the lantern light. All I see is a black void where his face should be, surrounded by what looks like a wig from a Halloween costume of a serial killer.

A wave of pain and dizziness forces my head back against the table.

"Please," I say again. "Melanie..."

"Is that her name? Very beautiful. Change the spelling —*Melania*—and it means 'darkness.' Did you know that?"

"Please..."

He hammers his fist against the table with a loud bang, so close his knuckles brush my coverall. It's then that I notice they've removed my utility belt, but not my boots— bad news with a little good news thrown in.

"Enough with that nonsense," he says. "I can't stand when you people plead for things. You're just lucky none of us are partial to boys. As for the girl, well, you can forget about her, Mr. Knight-in-Shining-Caked-Blood. She's meat."

I close my eyes and try to control my panicked breathing. My stomach hurts, and I'm nauseated, probably from hunger, though the gas fumes aren't helping. How long have I been out? It's dark in the warehouse, which means the windows are either boarded up, or the sun is warming up some other part of the globe.

If it's nighttime, I'm in serious trouble.

"I can get weapons," I say. "Give you wha-whatever you want."

The guy goes rigid suddenly, puffing his chest and standing as erect as a butler. I expect him to curse or spit at me, but instead he holds out his open palm to shake my hand.

I glance at it. Then I study his face to see if he's joking.

"Oh, that's right," he says. "You're tied to the table." Retracting his hand, he clears his throat. "We haven't been formally introduced. The name is Sanders, like the fried chicken guy. Colonel Sanders, get it? Everyone just calls me the Colonel now. Not without well-earned respect."

Yeah, right. Well-earned respect that comes from calling your friends names like "faggot" when you feel insecure about something.

The Colonel points at Bandanna. "This gentleman over here is Olin; couldn't think of a nickname for him, though he always wears a bandanna so I call him 'faggy bandanna-wearing gentleman'"—Olin smiles at this—"while this hirsute and debonair *caballero* over here"—he swings his finger at the man who had driven the Jeep—"is Russell, but we call him Wheels because he loves to bitch and moan if we don't let him drive the Wrangler."

The Colonel points at me. "And you, young squire, what is your name and family crest?"

I ignore his stupid mannerisms and stutter out what I can.

"K-Kip," I say, unable to control my shivering now. It's only going to sap my strength. I need to compose myself, but I'm in the grip of a panic attack, which hasn't happened since I was a kid. Thoughts of Melanie and my father and the antibiotics in my pack swirl maddeningly in my head.

The Colonel chuckles.

"Kip," he says, lowering his face—and his stinking, pube-like beard—over mine. "What kind of a wussy name is that?"

"Short for—for Kevin," I say. "Melanie. Where is she? What did you do to her?"

"Nothing yet. But I told you. She's meat." Then, with a

mocking squint and an equally mocking voice, he says, "What is she, anyway, your girlfriend? How sweet."

As I lie there shivering, he struts over to the other table, waves Bandanna aside, and picks out an instrument. When he comes back, he holds it over me just right so the blade flashes in the lantern's glow as he twists it.

I've never seen a scalpel up close. Never knew they could be so sharp. It looks like it could slice a diamond in half. But the blade isn't what scares me. It's the small size of it. A hunting knife would have told a different, and more predictable, story. The scalpel, however, is tiny in his bearish hand. This tells me the Colonel is going to take his sweet time with whatever torture he has planned.

"Here's what's going to happen, Kipper. Mind if I call you that?"

He actually waits for me to answer. My mouth is clamped shut, and I'm breathing so hard I can feel my nostrils stretching. I never look away from the scalpel as I gasp a reply.

"Yes."

"Yes, you *do* mind?"

"No."

"No, what?" he says.

His bushy eyebrows shoot up in amusement. This isn't about finding my stash and surviving. It's about having fun, passing the time, showing off to his buddies—both of who, strangely enough, remain completely silent.

I give him what he wants.

"No, sir."

"Very good. Now, this here is a scalpel. See these nicks and scratches?" He holds it over my face so I can study two nicks in the blade. "They're from hitting bones during the cutting process. I'm no doctor, you see, and sometimes my hands shake."

He holds the scalpel over my face. It's perfectly steady. A few seconds pass before he suddenly shakes it, forcing me to squeeze my eyes shut so I don't lose one.

"Oops! Almost got ya, Kipper!"

He chuckles. I glare at him, breathing through clenched teeth.

"Just stop," I say.

He ignores me. Now he's just standing there, studying my midsection like he's wondering which part of it to slice open first.

"The spleen, I gather, is located between the hypothalamus and the trachea," he says, either completely insane or having the time of his life, "which leads me to believe that a quarter-staff incision beneath the right circadian nerve structure—no, that's not right. Maybe if I cut from the balls up..."

He approaches me, blade extended, aimed at my crotch.

"Okay, okay," I say, pausing him. "I can take you to my stash. But my father's inside. He's armed. He'll shoot you, but—but not if you let me get him out of there."

The Colonel's arms cross over his chest, one hand twiddling the scalpel.

"So we just let you and your daddy go, is that it?"

I lick my lips. Maybe I'm getting somewhere. "I'll make you a deal. Let me and Melanie go into the house. We'll convince my dad to leave unarmed, and then the three of us will disappear. You can have the house and everything in it. It's yours, and no one has to die."

The Colonel taps his chin with the scalpel's blunt end, taking on a pensive look.

"Very idealistic," he says. "So, let's say I agree to let you,

Papa Smurf, and little Robin Hood-in-a-Skirt go scampering away into the woods together. What's to say you won't come back later to mess with my affairs?"

"Because it's too risky," I say. "There are three of you, all carrying guns. But I'll be unarmed with only an old man and a scared girl."

Something I said causes Wheels to launch himself into a standing position. He is easily taller than six feet.

"She ain't just a scared girl," Wheels says. "Someone trained her. I saw how she held that bow and went for that arrow. Besides, I called dibs on her—"

The Colonel cuts him off. "Noted, *capitán*. You've convinced me not to turn my life around and protect the innocent children after all, which I deeply appreciate."

Shaking his head and swearing under his breath, Wheels lowers himself onto the crate. Bandanna watches him, chuckling.

"Innocent children," Bandanna says. "That's rich."

Wheels lets out a frustrated grunt.

As I make sense of what has just happened, I feel a pang of hope. Their way of interacting with each other—the awkward displays of masculinity; the minor bouts of distrust, like the Colonel saying he used to work in the FBI; Wheels thinking the Colonel would just give away a girl he had already claimed—tells me that these guys are new to capturing survivors. They have no set of rules, no protocol in place. The nicks on the scalpel are most likely a lie meant to scare me.

This is all a game, a chance for them to outdo each other, maybe experiment with different styles and attitudes. That would explain the Colonel's childish arrogance and his stupid nicknames, and the way Wheels and Bandanna just stand there, waiting to see what happens next.

If I'm right, then that makes me a player—which also means I can win.

Or at least cheat.

"Who was he?" I ask the Colonel as he again makes his way to the metal instruments on the table. "The man you threw to the infected yesterday."

"You were watching us, eh? Or do you consult with owls, young Kip?"

He lifts a ballpeen hammer. I wince at the thought of the hammer's blunt tip causing gruesome damage to one of my testicles.

"For your information, he was my half-brother," the Colonel says, lowering the hammer and picking up a pair of scissors that squeaks as he flexes it. "My mother's bastard child from the fag lover she took before my old man made an honest woman out of her. Bobby was always trying to tell me what to do, how to run things."

"You killed your own brother?" I say.

He shrugs as if to say, *What else could I do?*

"Sure I did. You see, his last name was Lee, so everyone started calling him General, like the great General Robert E. Lee, the old Civil War guy. Since a general ranks higher than a colonel—"

Bandanna snickers at this. The Colonel, still holding the scissors, grins and shrugs again in a gesture of helplessness. It's obvious he's enjoying the attention.

Wheels, oblivious, has taken off one of his boots and is scratching the skin between his toes, emitting a foul smell. He's probably heard this story a million times.

"So what was I to do to correct this injustice?" the Colonel says, directing his words at Bandanna, the only person in his private audience who seems amused. "The bald-headed asshole thinks he can start bossing me around just because *he's* a general and I'm a lowly colonel?"

The Colonel is distracted as he tells the story. I use the opportunity to finger the knots binding my wrists. One of them feels loose, and I begin to pick at it.

Until I find Wheels standing over me.

"Want to lose a finger?" he says.

His voice comes out low and secretive. It sounds more like an offer than a threat, which means he is eager for the opportunity to hurt me. The man is clearly a psychopath.

My hands go loose and drop to the table.

"Hey, what's going on over there?" the Colonel asks, striding over.

He grabs Wheels by the front of his shirt, backs him up against the stack of shelves, and holds the open scissors against his neck, like he might snip his Adam's apple in half.

"I was in the middle of a story about my dear brother," the Colonel says. "Have you no heart? The man is dead!"

Bandanna convulses with laughter. I watch and listen for subtle messages in their confrontation.

"Let go of me," Wheels says to the Colonel, angry but calm.

"I will, but only if you play nice. This is *my* prisoner. You get the girl after Olin has his fun, which should only be about thirty seconds after he starts, like last time."

More raucous laughter from Bandanna. Maybe they *have* taken prisoners—a girl, it sounds like. My hope sinks.

"...then you can fatten her up all you want, my dear *capitán*."

These words make it sink even more.

I consider everything the Colonel has just said. It seems strange that Bandanna would go first when Wheels already "called dibs" on Melanie, unless the Colonel's use of the phrase "fatten her up" means that Wheels claimed her for something other than sex.

"Well, I, for one, think it's cutting time," the Colonel says, releasing Wheels. "Enough chit-chat, unless we're talking addresses and mailbox numbers." He turns to me and holds the open scissors above my groin. "Well, Kipper? Have anything to disclose?"

He makes a *snip snip* sound with the blades. Every muscle in my body clenches.

If I tell him what he wants, it probably won't change his plans. He'll kill me anyway. And why not? At that point, I'd be a risk and nothing more.

I see only one option left.

"You won't get anything from me," I say, meeting the Colonel's eyes. He pinches them in curiosity. "If Melanie is just meat and there's nothing I can do for her, then all I have to lose is my life. And I don't care about that anymore. So you have two options."

"Oh?" he says. "Kipper is giving me *options*. Look at that."

"Yeah," I say, "well, you won't even get those if you touch me. Or I could take you to my stash. That's the only way you'll find it. Up to you."

"Hmm." The Colonel pets his beard with one hand, snaps the scissors with the other. His next question catches me off guard. "Are you left-handed or right-handed, Mr. Kip?"

"Left," I say, which is a lie. A natural reaction. I only hope it's the right one. I mimic a tone of regret. "Why? What are you going to do?"

"Hold his left hand down," the Colonel tells Wheels.

Wheels grabs my left wrist and pins it to the table.

"What are you gonna do?" I say, breathing hard.

The Colonel holds up the scissors and studies them.

"Nah," he says and flings them away—a ringing sound of metal against metal as they crash into a shelf. "I know what I need. Good old trusty friend of mine."

He goes back to the table, picks up the scalpel, and brings it over.

He's standing to my left now, next to Wheels, who is using both of his hands to pin down my wrist, even though I'm not struggling. The sharp ache in my skull has expanded into a full-on hurricane of pounding agony. Sweat, cold as ice, drips down the sides of my face.

I keep quiet and try to breathe steadily. No matter what happens, I can't crack.

Pain is just a signal, my father told me once, in the early months of the Outbreak when I tried to get out of a daily workout session by complaining about sore muscles. *A message your nerves are sending to your brain. It's background music you can learn to tune out...*

"I'm going to test you," the Colonel says. "If what you say is true, and torture won't be enough to get you to spill the beeswax, I'll know in a matter of minutes."

"If I scream?" I ask him, holding his gaze.

He wags the scalpel at me. "You scream, and I'll know you're weak. I'll keep right on going until you tell me where your stash is located, and what kinds of booby traps your old man has set up around the house. I find out you're lying, and when I get back, we'll have a second date in Hell, you and I."

"You won't get anything," I tell him. "You're just wasting time and daylight."

Bandanna emerges from the darkness to my right. He leans over me.

"So get it over with," he says in his raspy voice. "Save yourself the trouble. Tell us where it is."

I spit in his face—pale, foamy flecks that make him recoil, blinking and muttering curses. My body tenses in anticipation of his response. He pulls back an arm to slap me, but the Colonel reaches across the table and levels the scalpel at him. Bandanna freezes.

"What the fuck, Colonel?"

"*My* prisoner, remember?"

Bandanna nods and backs away. Crossing his arms, he leans against a stack and watches while the Colonel focuses on my clenched hand.

"Open sesame," he says. "Let me see those fingernails. Or maybe you're too scared. Is that it, Kipper? Should we maybe talk about your house instead?"

I raise my hand, but the fingers remain bent inward against my palm.

All but one of them.

I extend my middle finger, a symbolic *fuck you* I want badly to say out loud.

"Your move," I say instead.

The Colonel chuckles, shaking his greasy head. "You know what, Kipper? I like you. If it makes you feel any better, I think you could have been one of us."

I ignore him and concentrate on the darkness above us. I try to project myself into it so my consciousness is no more than a distant satellite orbiting my body, dead space between the two. A barrier to keep away the pain. My father tried to teach me this technique once.

I never got the hang of it.

The Colonel starts on my middle finger. I feel a tickle as the blade slips between the nail and the skin beneath it. When it severs the connective tissue binding the two, the pain is so great I'm amazed by it.

My spine rises off the table as my back takes on the shape of Melanie's compound bow.

Pain is just a signal. A message. Background music.

A silent scream claws its way out of my chest. It beats the walls of my throat, desperate to break free. I swallow it down.

"Thattaboy, Kipper," the Colonel says.

He flicks something away. My fingernail, probably.

Then he starts on my ring finger, again, slipping the blade under my nail.

Oh God, holy shit, the pain!

It's just a signal, a message, background music. You can tune it out. You can tune it out, just a signal, a message, background music, like in those elevators, the people standing around, tuning out the pain, the music, the background elevators...

Blinding, sparkling pain—stars against the blackness. I thrust myself toward them, reaching for the escape that lies beyond.

Another finger—another nail...another journey to those stars.

Laughing. They're laughing at me.

I flatten my back against the table, holding back tears, gritting my teeth in silence.

Another finger—my thumb, this time—gets torn open at the tip, and new stars are birthed against the darkness. My teeth are clenched so tightly together that I wonder if I'll ever be able to open my mouth. The phrase, *Pain is just a signal,* becomes more rapid, harder to hold on to, a flailing rope I try to grab like I'm drowning, and the phrase is my lifeline.

If I let go, I'll sink into the pain. I'll let its current carry me away, and I'll scream just to be able to breathe again. I'll howl and beg and yell for the Colonel to stop and let me go, for the men to go raid my house at 113 Exeter Road, Peltham Park, NH 03812, my father be damned.

Melanie takes my hand.

I don't see her. She is a phantom resting its warm weight against me.

It doesn't matter, she whispers into my mind, filling it. *But I do. I matter because you love me. The pain is nothing. It doesn't exist.*

But I do.

That's when it comes out of me.

"More," I tell Wheels and the Colonel, and suddenly I'm hysterical, free, my body shaking like I'm possessed, cannibalizing the screams and shitting them out as laughter. "More, more, more, more, more, more...!"

Laughter. That's the secret. Dad had it wrong. I'm laughing, and suddenly the pain isn't so bad, because that's the music right there.

I laugh at them, not with amusement, but with the ravenous hunger that fuels the infected—hunger not for food, but for more reasons to laugh at their stupid, worthless plans, and their stupid, worthless fucking lives that are no more than a virus, the weakest kind.

"I'll be goddamned," the Colonel says over my maniacal laughter, though he isn't laughing the slightest bit. Neither is Wheels, who's glaring at me beneath furrowed brows—or Bandanna, who's standing nearby with his mouth forming an O of surprise. Finally, my laughter dies away, and now the Colonel is the one chuckling.

"What a trooper. Look at this guy," he says.

The pain in my hand is excruciating.

So this is what it feels like to have your fingernails torn off.

I want to swing my fist into the Colonel's grinning face,

but the rope binding me to the table makes it so I can only twitch in helpless rage.

"You gave your word," I manage to growl at him.

The Colonel wipes sweat off my forehead with one hand, a motion almost fatherly in nature. "That I did, brave Kipper. That I did."

He motions for the others to undo my binds. Wheels and Bandanna get to it—grudgingly, I sense from their expressions, but silent as a pair of mimes.

The infected shuffle and moan outside the warehouse. One begins to pound his fist against the wall.

Ignoring them, the Colonel waits for his men to finish. He pulls my gloves out of his back pocket and throws them at me, probably to stanch the bleeding.

"You're going to show me where your stash is," he tells me as I slip on the gloves, wincing at the pain. "That's step number one. Then you're going to enter your humble abode like nothing bad ever happened to you in your whole life.

"Here's the fun part: you're going to come back out carrying your father's head ten minutes after you go in. Not a single minute later. Do you comprehend my vibe, dear Kip? Processing our palaver, so to speak?"

Despite his weird mannerisms, the Colonel's voice is now flat and serious, his face even more so. If this is a game, then it's a totally new level for both of us.

"Or what?" I say. "What happens if I don't come out in ten minutes?"

He leans toward me, clamps his hand around my neck, and draws me close. Our foreheads touch, and I have to endure his nauseating breath.

"Any funny business while you're in that house, Kipper, and I'll inflict so much pain on your little girlfriend that ripping off *her* fingernails will be just the foreplay."

10

On my way out of the warehouse, I see why the entire place reeks of gasoline.

The Colonel and his men have gathered a stockpile of it in the center of the main storage area. There are entire stacks of shelves loaded with red, five-gallon polyethylene cans. I see them only briefly in what little light Bandanna casts from the lantern as we walk by, but I can tell there are at least four full stacks holding twenty or more cans on each shelf.

It's a rough estimate, but at the very least—assuming the cans are full—we're talking about a few hundred gallons of gasoline. It's the equivalent of a treasure chest full of gold coins for someone in pre-Outbreak society.

I dwell on these numbers as the Colonel leads me across the main storage area. My wrists are bound together by twine at the small of my back. More of it ties my ankles together, giving me enough slack so I can walk but not run. I shuffle along, taking in every detail I can, expecting to emerge into sunlight soon. Then maybe I'll find out where this place is located.

Instead of leading me to the exit, the Colonel takes me to see Melanie.

She's sitting on the floor in the corner, her back against the wall and her knees drawn up to her chest. In front of her is an empty stack. Sandwiched between the two, she looks tiny and vulnerable, like a homeless girl out on a cold night begging for change.

"Melanie," I say.

Bandanna blows out the lantern, sets it on the floor, and turns on a pocket flashlight. He shines the beam in her eyes, making her wince. Her face looks puffy and her hair is a ratty, sweat-soaked mess that hangs in shreds over her eyes. Her right hand is suspended above her shoulder, dangling from a pair of handcuffs attached to a metal loop embedded in the wall.

"Kip?" she says.

"Are you okay? Did they hurt you?"

"I'll live," she says.

The Colonel puts a hand on my shoulder to discourage me from getting any closer. I twist away from his grasp. He responds by grabbing the neck of my coverall and yanking me back.

"Not so fast, Kipper."

I imagine sticking the barrel of my Glock into his mouth and pulling the trigger.

"Melanie is going to need a babysitter while we're out shopping," the Colonel tells me with a pat on the shoulder. "Lucky for us, Wheels has volunteered to keep an eye on her. Isn't that right, Wheels?"

"Fuckin' right it's right," Wheels says, fixing his soulless eyes on mine. The words *fatten her up* hit me again with their ominous meaning.

"I thought Olin was supposed to be first," I say, looking at Bandanna.

"Now that's a damned good point," Bandanna says. "Why don't I stay behind with her?"

The Colonel smacks me hard against the back of my head. Melanie whimpers at the sight of me stumbling to regain my balance.

"That'll teach you to mess around," the Colonel says before addressing Bandanna. "She'll be here when we return, unless Kip fails to follow instructions, in which case, the girl may soon be missing certain parts of her body. Not any parts you'd be interested in, *capitán*."

Bandanna accepts this with a grateful nod.

"You hear that, Kipper?" the Colonel says. "Won't be any need for even a single hair on her stinky head to get plucked if things go according to plan. But, if for some reason I don't return to my humble abode by sunrise, I've given Wheels permission to engage in certain delights of a carnal nature with your little girlfriend. And believe you me, sittin' in a tree, when Wheels is involved, the term 'carnal delight' takes on a whole new meaning." He snaps his fingers at Wheels. "Show him what I mean."

Wheels digs a small flashlight out of his pocket, shines it up at his own face, and grins. This is the first time I've seen him open his mouth wide enough to reveal what's inside.

I wish he had kept it shut. His yellow front teeth are the stuff of nightmares, each one sharpened into a fine point that makes his entire mouth resemble that of a great white shark.

He must have already revealed his gruesome mouth to Melanie. When I look at her again, the expression on her face is one of pure dread. She knows as well as I do that Wheels is a cannibal.

"Let us commence, shall we?" the Colonel says, which prompts Wheels to click off his flashlight and turn toward Melanie.

Bandanna also turns his off, leaving Melanie and Wheels in the same pocket of darkness near the wall. Not being able to see them launches me into a panic.

"Get away from her," I shout. "Keep him away!"

Bandanna approaches me. He lifts his hands, and I see something stretched between them, maybe a length of fabric, though I can't tell for sure in the near-complete darkness.

The Colonel grips my shoulder again.

"Easy now, Kipper."

The blindfold erases my sight as Bandanna ties it around my head, his movements brutish and painful, his low laughter entering my ear like crushed glass.

THE BLINDFOLD COMES OFF ONLY after the Jeep has taken us beyond sight of the warehouse, though I'm still convinced the Colonel and his friends rarely take prisoners. It's a stupid mistake on their part. If they had been smarter or more experienced, they would have kept the blindfold on much longer. We're not even out of the industrial complex yet, which gives me a chance to memorize the route.

A layer of gray-white clouds covers the evening sky. There are maybe two hours of daylight left, which means I wasn't unconscious for very long. It also means that if I plan to escape and come back for Melanie, I'll have to do it quickly or risk having to travel by night.

The Colonel sits with me in the back seat, slumped against the door so he can face me. My Glock is in his right hand. He keeps it at rest between his legs, not even aiming it.

Once we are out of the industrial complex, I try to mark my whereabouts in relation to other buildings—mostly houses—that I hope to recognize. But we're not in any part of Peltham Park I've ever seen before. I try not to make it obvious that I'm scouting the area. Mostly I keep my head down, faking an expression of utter defeat, while using my peripheral vision to study my surroundings.

Five minutes into the ride, the Colonel launches into a speech that begins with, "You know why I love this town?" As he speaks, I count the different turns we make to get back on Route 1. When he starts talking about the sexy waitress at what used to be his favorite diner, my thoughts turn to Melanie, trapped in the warehouse with Wheels, and the way the darkness engulfed her when the last flashlight was turned off.

I try not to think about it as I keep marking turns and distance traveled.

The trip is a painful one. Bandanna can't drive worth a damn and hits every pothole he can before getting on a dirt road that takes us through a heavily forested area. This is a part of Peltham Park I never knew existed, where large, lonely old houses pop up behind the trees, looking empty and barren, the yards plagued with weeds and brambles.

"You wouldn't believe the valuable shit we found in these old houses," Bandanna says, following it up with an admiring whistle. "Barely had to kill anyone to get it, too."

The Colonel points at one of the houses. "Lovely lesbian couple lived in that one over there."

He describes what he made them do to each other while he watched. I won't recount it here, but the story involves torture and sadism on a level I wouldn't have expected even from him.

Throughout the trip, they never ask for directions, only the name of my road. The Colonel knows Peltham Park as if he's spent all of his life here. Maybe he has. He tells Bandanna where to go—mostly along dirt roads through the woods—and before I know it, we're on the main road leading toward my house.

"It's that one," I say.

Bandanna points at my house as it emerges from behind a wall of trees. "That one right there?"

"Yeah."

The Colonel throws a glance over his shoulder. If my hands weren't tied together, I'd snatch the gun right off his lap and put a slug through his head, no problem. Then I'd blast Bandanna's skull into bits before he could even slam on the brakes. I settle for pulling against my binds in silent rage.

"Windows are completely sealed and the roof is clear," Bandanna says. "Nowhere to snipe from. Nothing to worry about."

He continues listing off details to prove we're in no danger as we approach. I have to admit, he knows what he's talking about. It's clear these men have seized fortified houses before, even if they didn't take prisoners afterward. That just means they killed everyone inside.

We creep up the length of my driveway and park near the double doors of the garage. The Colonel shoves me out of the back seat, keeping the gun trained on my head.

Like other houses on my street, ours was built against a small hill. The backyard is actually a wooded slope that juts upward. If you face the two garage doors, to the left, you'll see the hill, and to the right is the front yard, which slopes gently downward. Against the hill, between its base and the garage, is a narrow path about four feet wide that lets you walk around to the back of the house.

Edging that channel of space is a granite wall my father built against the earth. He also made a granite footpath leading around back to the deck on the other end of the house.

The Colonel and Bandanna undo my binds and follow me to the beginning of the path. Around the corner is the hatch built into one of the garage windows. Less than twenty-four hours have passed since I first crawled out of it.

They follow me around the corner.

"Nice and hidden," the Colonel says, admiring the hatch.

Bandanna has brought the M16 and keeps it trained on my back as I stick the key into the padlock and twist.

The Colonel pushes me aside and runs his hand along the surface of the hatch. It's just a flap of heavy steel that drapes the window, a handle built into it and another built into the wall so you can chain the two together. But he's opening and closing it and tonguing his teeth like he plans to build one just like it. The black rose on his neck creeps upward as he stretches himself to touch the hinges running along the top.

"In ten minutes, you emerge from this hatch like the snake that you are, Kipper," the Colonel says, "and if I see you carrying anything other than your old man's head, it's rat-tat-tat time for you, *comprende*?"

We lock eyes, mine carrying rage that must be obvious; his showing a mixture of grandiosity and relief, like he can't believe how easy this has been.

"Fuck you," I say.

Bandanna raises the M16. The Colonel waves it back down, nodding and smiling at me.

"Thattaboy," he says. "Now get in there and bring me that head, Kipper."

I turn to lift the hatch when he clasps my shoulder and spins me around. With a stern look, he jabs a finger at my face.

"Don't think I'm stupid," he says, dark eyes boring into mine. He's more serious now than I've seen him so far. "I won't give you the chance to snipe me from the windows. I won't be visible from the rooftop. And if you're not back here in ten minutes, I will break down these walls and come after you, and Melanie will die a painful, biblical death. You got that, Kip?"

His use of my name, instead of that nickname Kipper, chills me right down to the marrow. I nod once at him and turn toward the hatch.

"You've got a steel heart, young squire," he says and pats my shoulder.

Then he holds up the hatch, and I climb inside.

THE FAMILIAR, fungal smell of the garage fills my nose, reminding me of my parents.

Using my flashlight, I make my way past the cluttered shelves, the busted minivan, and the tools all over the floor. Everything is exactly how I left it. My hands shake as I fumble for the keys. When I open the door, I'm greeted by a sour stink almost like that of my high school's locker room after soccer practice.

"Hello?" I call out when I see the couch is empty.

The smell gets worse as I make my way to my parents' bedroom.

"Dad?" I say as I open the door and peer inside.

My father is curled up on the bed he and my mother had

once shared, his skin a sickly pallor and coated with sweat. He's in drastically worse shape than he was yesterday. His eyes are open just a crack, barely enough for me to see his pupils roll toward me. In his hand is a framed photograph of our family. On the bedside table is a 9mm pistol I imagine is fully loaded.

"Dad," I say again, gripping his free hand. "Can you hear me?"

His breath is foul and his eyes are as yellow as corn. The skin around them crinkles with emotion. He's barely breathing, and his voice comes out an abrupt whisper.

"Kip?"

"I'm so sorry, Dad," I say as I drop to my knees next to the bed, still clasping his ice-cold hand. "I failed. I don't have the medicine. I'm sorry."

His voice scrapes out of him. "Doesn't—matter. Too—late."

"Just hold on." I blink away tears. "There are men outside. They want us out of here."

Hearing this, Dad's brow tightens in a look of cold rage.

"Why don't—they enter?"

"They think you're armed and ready to shoot them. They want proof that you're not a threat to them. But I won't do it."

A sudden surge of vitality comes into him. He grips my hand.

"Yes. Give it to them. Make it—hurt."

"I can't kill you, Dad. That's what they want. I can't do it."

"Do it for—for Mom," he says. "She wants you—to live. I'm dead, Kip. *Dead.*"

"But I can kill them. I can snipe them from—"

"No!"

He tosses my hand aside and coughs violently. I wipe

phlegm from the corner of his mouth. His trembling has stopped. His eyes remain open.

I'm sure he's dead. Then his eyes roll toward the bedside table and the gun lying on its surface.

"Listen to me now," he says, "and do exactly as I say…"

I SIT against the closed bedroom door, my dad alone in the bedroom. The gun goes off less than ten seconds after I closed the door and slid down its length to the carpet. My father is dead.

They must have heard the shot outside. The Colonel will assume I went through with the plan, buying me a few more minutes.

As soon as it's done, I push myself up and open the door.

Dad shot himself in the heart just as he had said he would. It was part of his plan. He's dead by the time I make it back to the bed. I kiss his forehead and tell him I love him, but I don't dwell on my loss. That will come later.

With hurried movements, I dig out a hunting knife from the bedside table—my father put one in practically every room—and go to work.

When I'm finished, my hands covered in blood I'll never be able to wash off, I run into the room where I packed my bug-out bag the day before. I throw open the closet doors, drop to my knees, and slide a heavy shoebox toward me.

11

"That you, Kipper?"

The Colonel has heard the hatch over the garage window slam back into place. I stand facing the granite wall against the hill, listening to the crunching of leaves and twigs as he and Bandanna make their way out of the woods, followed by the scraping of shoes against pavement. I imagine the Colonel crouched behind the Jeep for cover while Bandanna aims the M16 at me in case I come out shooting.

"It's me," I say. "I have what you want."

I look down at my hands, which carry my father's severed head. Studying the cold mask of his face, the eyes turned up in their sockets, I have to hold back tears, though not because I'm worried about crying in front of the Colonel. I need clear vision for what I'm about to do next.

There is a frag grenade stuffed inside my father's mouth. I've cut an opening through the corner of his lips and into his cheek so the strike lever can escape once I pull the pin, which I do by lowering my mouth to his, clamping my teeth around the pin, and yanking it. My thumb remains pressed against the lever to keep the explosion at bay.

For now.

"You're going to walk around the garage very slowly," the Colonel says from the driveway, "and then you're going to turn around so I can make sure you're not strapped. I see even a flash of gunmetal, Kipper, and you're going down the gravity elevator to concrete land. In other words, I will drop you to the fucking ground, you got that?"

"Just don't shoot," I say. "I'm coming out."

I kiss my father's forehead and ease my way around the garage. The two men are standing in front of the Jeep. The Colonel holds the Glock at his side like he isn't worried about a thing. He even wears a confident smile. Bandanna is in a combat stance, holding the weapon and aiming through the sights with one eye closed.

"Spin around slowly," the Colonel says. "No sudden moves."

I hug my father's head so his face is pressed against my chest, the grenade's lever jabbing one of my ribs. This keeps it down for now.

I turn ever so slowly—probably more slowly than they expect.

"You made me kill my own father," I say as I turn. "He didn't do anything to you."

With my back to them, I let go of the lever. It pops open.

I have five seconds.

"He just wanted to be left alone," I say.

Four seconds.

The Colonel sighs dramatically. "*C'est la vie*, Kipper. We can't always get what we want."

Three seconds.

"He wanted me to give you a message," I say, facing them again.

The Colonel is aiming the Glock at me.

I was right. They never intended to let me go.

Two seconds.

"Oh?" the Colonel says, "and what's that?"

"Go to hell."

I toss my father's head at their feet.

Bandanna fires the M16 but misses me as I duck around the garage.

Perfect timing. The explosion slams the garage doors with a hollow boom. It sends shock waves that rattle my body even as I land behind cover. There's a metal ripping sound that must be the Jeep being torn apart, accompanied by a roar that reminds me of thunder.

As I lie on my stomach, hands covering my head, I listen for footsteps—one or both men running for cover. But all I hear is the pattering of debris falling back to the ground.

I spit out bits of dirt that have gotten into my mouth and roll onto my back. All I see is smoke. I sit up and grab a rock in case I need to throw it at someone.

No one emerges from the haze, and I don't hear a single shout or cry of pain.

I still need to make sure they're dead. When the smoke clears, I immediately see the dusty, broken remains of Bandanna propped against the granite wall, his right side completely torn apart.

The Colonel is in the woods several yards away, in about the same terrible shape as Bandanna. He's lying facedown, both legs missing. Maybe he turned to run away at the last second. I can barely see the tattoo on his neck from all the dust and damage.

I check his pockets, hoping for keys to the warehouse.

Nothing. I check Bandanna as well, but all I get is blood on my hands.

Nothing inside the remains of the Jeep, either. The keys are probably lying in the woods somewhere, little more than bits of twisted metal now.

I race back into the garage, where I left one of the emergency packs my father and I pre-packed long ago for situations in which we had to make a hurried escape. It has all the basics for a few days of survival outside the house. The 9mm is on the floor next to it, along with a few ammo clips. I take all of it and leave through the busted garage door.

The evening sky is darkening into night. The next several hours will be dangerous, more so than anything I've attempted so far. Already I can hear moans coming from the woods behind our house.

I shoulder the pack and run as fast as I can toward town, only my compass for guidance.

When my mother worked as a pre-school teacher, she suffered from fatigue that made her irritable and scatterbrained toward the end of each shift. She saw a doctor who prescribed stimulants, the same stuff they give kids with ADHD. After the Outbreak, my father took those drugs and split them up among the different emergency packs and medical kits we kept around the house. His thinking was that if the house came under attack, the stimulants would help us delay sleep while we defended the place.

An attack like that never happened, so I'm sure my pack holds at least two of those pink pills somewhere inside. I'm familiar with their effect already. I stole a few sophomore year to help me study for a final exam.

As I jog, I dig through the pack with my good hand. The

other grips the 9mm despite the constant sting from its missing fingernails. Fortunately, the medical supplies are near the top of the pack. Keeping a steady pace, I tear open the kit, find the bag containing the pills, and pop both into my mouth. Then I stuff the medical kit back inside, dig out a water bottle, and take a long sip to wash them down.

I'm not sure if taking the pills on an empty stomach will make me throw up, so I keep searching the pack until I find PowerBars in a front pocket. I wolf down two of them and immediately feel better.

Once the food settles and the pills take effect, I'm able to bolt through the backwoods of Peltham Park without much complaint from my body. The pain is something I've learned to ignore.

Still, I wish the explosion had spared the Jeep. With its off-roading ability, I could have stayed off the main roads and cut my ETA down to just twenty minutes. Judging by how long it took me to get there by foot the day before, I know Melanie is at least five hours away.

I see my first group of infected after an hour of running. I take cover behind a tree and watch them shuffle and lurch like sleepwalkers in the dimming light. There are three of them, two males and a female, but with night settling over us, I can't tell if they're late-stagers or not. Hopefully they're as blind as bats.

I could go around them, but instead I opt for a diversionary tactic. I pick up rocks until I have a handful and start tossing them at a dead tree about twenty yards away. The stimulants help me focus on the tree and nothing else, and I manage to land most of my throws.

With the infected now moving toward the source of the noise, I sneak past them, continuing to launch rocks.

But I screw up.

I'm so focused on diverting the three infected that I don't see the fourth until I almost walk right into it.

It's a child. A little girl with knotted blonde hair.

I stop a foot in front of her, right hand still clutching a rock I was about to throw. The girl is shockingly dirty, covered in dried mud and leaves. There's a long, thin branch stuck to the side of her head.

She's in bad shape. Her skin is a pale, semi-translucent sheet that wraps tightly against her bones, covered in sores and scrapes. A milky cast over one eye tells me she is at least partially blind. She can't be more than three years old.

I drop the rock. I don't have what it takes to bash in her head. Now I'm not sure what to do.

Can she even see me?

Her nostrils flare, detecting my smell. She opens her mouth and releases a shrill moan that sounds disturbingly like a healthy little girl crying because she's lost.

I run past her, avoiding her grasping fingers. A quick glance over my shoulder tells me the other three have heard and are now hot on my trail.

Like most infected, they can't run very fast. But there's no telling what kind of stamina they possess. I've seen infected stand in one place for longer than I thought humanly possible. One guy stood outside my house for more than thirty hours because he caught sight of me on the roof. If that incident is any indication, these three—not four, since I imagine the girl got left behind—will probably chase me for hours.

I book it out of there. I'm still running when the remaining light bleeds out of the sky, leaving the forest dark. It becomes a nightmare of black shapes I think are trees, though my imagination paints them as something much worse. The infected make a racket as they continue to chase me. No doubt my scent is leading them right along.

That gives me an idea.

I stop by a tree with a mess of branches sticking out of it. All of this running has drenched my clothes with sweat. I throw down my pack and rest my gun on top of it, then proceed to rip open the buttoned part of my Nomex suit that covers my chest. Beneath it, I'm wearing a polyester shirt. I tear it off in a flurry of movement.

The fabric is damp with sweat and probably smells a lot like me. I sling it over a branch. The infected are close behind me. I can hear their clumsy footsteps rustling the underbrush.

I pick up the gun and my pack and sprint away at an angle, then swing around to catch them from behind.

The infected run past me, a flurry of inky silhouettes tumbling across the underbrush. Gripping the pistol, I dig out an LED flashlight from the pack's side pocket and wait a few moments longer.

I raise the flashlight, turned off for now, alongside my gun. My aim is shaky.

The infected attack the branch carrying my shirt, making snarling noises that sound like a pack of wolves tearing apart a helpless animal. I creep toward them, pop on the flashlight, and aim the pistol at the frenzied figures that suddenly appear in the beam.

One of the men has gotten caught in the branches, and the other two are trying to push him away to get to the shirt, which is also caught. Those two whirl around to face me. I shoot the closest one in the chest to push it back, then do the same to the other. They stagger. I use the opportunity to take better aim.

Headshots. Both of them. My father would be proud.

After I take out the one that had gotten caught in the branches, I button up my coverall, shoulder my pack, holster my pistol, and shine the flashlight at my compass to reorient myself.

I don't know how close I am to town, but I keep going.

The Colonel had set a deadline for his return. If he wasn't back by sunrise, Wheels could have his fun with Melanie. I recall the image of his sharp teeth, so much like those of a piranha.

I guzzle water and inhale another PowerBar, though my appetite has been killed by the stimulants.

And I keep running.

12

Whispers of daylight fill the sky.

Sunrise hasn't happened yet, but it will in less than an hour. I stopped checking my watch hours ago after almost tripping across an unseen branch. Time doesn't matter, anyway—daylight is my deadline.

The trip hasn't been easy. At this point, my feet are covered in patches of throbbing, wet pain—blisters that have formed and popped. It feels like I'm hobbling across a carpet of stinging jellyfish.

I make it to a familiar intersection on Route 1. To my left is the Exxon station where the Colonel worked once as a cashier.

Fuck him.

Melanie is all I think about as I force my legs to move. I find cover behind the wasted metal shell of a delivery truck tipped onto its side. From there, I study the intersection and the street that branches eastward toward the coast. It should take me to the industrial park where the warehouse is located.

Farther down that road, the infected aren't much of an issue. This area is residential, and as a result, there are more forested patches of land between buildings. I've learned to feel safe in areas with lots of trees. That feeling has never gone away.

I arrive at the warehouse minutes before sunrise. A steely blue light dominates the sky, not strong enough to cast shadows, but enough to see the broken windows of distant buildings inside the industrial park.

I reach the warehouse and stay away from the road in front. My knees burn from having to run while crouching, but I do this in case Wheels is armed with a sniper rifle. Taking the long way, out of necessity, I circle the building while keeping among my friends, the trees.

A chilling question hangs over me: What do I do next?

I'm at the edge of the loading area behind the warehouse, in a dirt lot where I take cover behind a row of massive tanks that were once red but are now a faded rust, the paint cracked and flaky. I look over the edge of one and study the building.

The Colonel and his men did an excellent job fortifying the place. They built barriers made of wooden boards, steel planks, and sand bags perfect for providing cover while shooting. They even erected barbed-wire fences around the personnel entrances to discourage invaders from barging through. The wide loading bay doors that once opened to admit the tail ends of trucks are covered in webs of stainless steel cables bolted in place around the edges. Looking up, I see lumpy shapes along the sloped rooftop—more sandbags stacked to make cover.

I know we used a door earlier to get outside. And I remember a heavy bang after they closed it. It'll be locked, and I don't have the proper tools for lock picking or hacking a steel chain. We never packed those into the emergency bags because there simply weren't enough of those tools to go around.

I don't see movement on the roof, so I make a run for it, my destination a low wall of sandbags halfway between me and the warehouse.

Something cuts the air next to me and smacks into the pavement.

I throw myself toward the sandbags and press against them. Did he shoot from the roof or a window I neglected to see? Either way, the good news is that he's shooting at me and not at Melanie.

The sandbag behind my head vibrates as another slug hits it. I flinch and try to flatten as much of myself against the ground as possible.

"You get up right now," Wheels shouts at me from above, "or your little girlfriend dies."

He's going to kill her anyway. Does he think I'm stupid?

Breathing hard, my chin scraping the pavement, I look for a better position of cover closer to the warehouse. His voice gives away an important detail of his location: namely that he's shooting from an elevated position higher than the first floor. From that elevation, he won't be able to shoot me as long as I'm pressed up against the building, not unless he stands at the edge of the roof or leans out of a window. If that happens, I'll put a bullet in him.

"I swear to Christ I'll do it," he shouts, and now it sounds like he's very high up, probably the rooftop.

I consider his threat. The man is clearly a psycho, but would he really kill Melanie right away? Or would he be smart and keep her hostage a while longer?

It's a tough call, but I make the assumption she's safe. Wheels probably knows by now that I got the best of the

Colonel, as well as Bandanna, who I'm pretty sure was their best marksman. If Wheels even has half a brain in that cannibal head of his, he won't waste the most precious resource and last line of defense he has: a girl I clearly love.

"You shoot her," I say in my loudest voice, "and you've got nothing. Your friends are dead. I'll have all the time in the world to hunt you down!"

"Is that right, Kip?"

There's amusement in his voice, and not the sort of arrogant, condescending amusement I'm used to from the Colonel. Wheels isn't fully confident about his situation. Maybe he has a trick up his sleeve.

"Take all the time out there you need," he says. "Hell, I even got something to keep you entertained in the meantime."

I hold my breath and wait. Then I hear it, a soft smack against the pavement next to the building, followed by a sizzling noise, and the firecrackers begin to go off, one after another.

I can hear Wheels laughing over the mini-explosions. It hits me that those fireworks might be how the Colonel and his men found us in the first place. Curse that old man in the window. If only we had passed him by.

Smoke. Those firecrackers are notorious for kicking up smoke. I already catch its heady, sulfuric stench. I look around the sandbags and see a cloud of it against the wall. It flashes bright orange with each pop.

A chorus of human moans and guttural grunts rises in every direction. Infected. They're coming to explore the noise. I can see flashes of movement in the trees—ruined bodies sprinting toward me, or at least lumbering quickly.

Wheels is still laughing. I chance a look at the roof and catch sight of him peeking out from behind a low wall of sandbags similar to mine, a hunting rifle propped against the top edge.

I fire the 9mm at him without taking close aim. The slug pings off the roof. He dips behind the sand bags, and I use that sliver of time to throw myself over my own wall of cover and sprint to the warehouse. Immediately, I flatten my back against the wall.

The last firecracker goes off. The smoke billows up, thick enough as it crosses his line of fire that I know I'm safe from his aim. I bolt along the wall, hook around the corner, and scan the unfamiliar terrain on this side.

This side of the warehouse is just as heavily fortified as the back. I see a door that I assume is the one we used earlier. It's the only one on this side of the building that isn't boarded up.

Of course it's locked—a steel deadbolt that requires a key. Shooting it won't do much good, either. It's the same brand my father and I used back home. Tough to break, even with a gun.

A hole has been drilled through the door at eye level. I look through it and see only darkness, and yet it feels like someone is staring back at me. An unlikely possibility. Even if Melanie has broken free of her bindings, I doubt she would be standing by this door just waiting for me to come knocking.

I hear a sharp yell from above, followed by gunfire.

Wheels.

What could he be shooting at now? Firing at the infected won't do him any good. Maybe he tripped and fired the rifle by accident? The roof is slanted, so it's possible. And that would explain the yell that was definitely his.

Sweat pours down my face. I'm cold and shivering now, gritting my teeth at the sudden wave of hopelessness that chills me to the bone. I've reached a dead end. The only option is to look for another way in, maybe around the front, something I missed before.

The moans grow louder, accompanied by the rustling of bodies moving through the woods, and finally the clapping of feet against pavement in the back lot.

The infected know I'm here. They're coming for me. I might as well use my gun on the door, though I'll have to lock it back up somehow once I get inside. Assuming the bullet even breaks through the lock.

I stand back several feet and grip the pistol in both hands.

A swarm of infected appears behind the warehouse. From the corner of my eye, I see them rounding the tanks, making a beeline toward me.

I place my finger on the trigger.

A naked man heads the pack of infected. He's about ten yards away, hands clawing toward me.

So close. They've gotten so close, so fast.

I curl my trigger finger. Press it against the metal.

I hear a click.

Releasing the trigger, I watch as the door handle turns. The door swings open.

My pistol goes up, ready to shoot at Wheels. I imagine him standing there with his own weapon raised.

It's Melanie.

"Get in," she says. "Hurry!"

The infected arrive.

I twist away as the naked man dives toward me. He misses by an inch. My back slams against the wall, followed by the back of my skull. The impact puts me in a daze.

Melanie's arm reaches around the doorframe and grabs the fabric of my coverall. She yanks me into a warm, dark room and slams the door shut as I land against concrete, everything suddenly black around me.

I push myself up and holster my pistol, eyes searching the darkness for Melanie. This part of the warehouse is stuffier than where I awoke the night before. The smell of gasoline, though still pervasive, is mixed with another smell that reminds me of an old, untended garden.

No time to explore smells. Wheels is probably running toward this very room.

"Where is he?" I ask the darkness in front of me. I have to shout over the battering the infected have unleashed against the building.

Melanie responds by cupping my face with both of her hands and kissing me.

"I'm so glad it's you," she says. "Are the others dead? Did you kill them?"

"Yeah, they're gone. But Wheels—"

"I hurt him. I don't think he's lucid."

"What?"

"Hold on."

Something scrapes against fabric. Her hand sliding into her pocket. A scratching noise is followed by a loud pop as Melanie lights a match. She holds it in the space between our faces.

A rifle shot from the main storage area startles us. Wheels is firing—but at what, exactly? Have the infected gotten inside?

Melanie blows out the match. I have to raise my voice to be heard over the pounding against the walls.

"You said he's not lucid. What does that mean? Is he infected?"

"No. I drugged him."

"How? Melanie, what—"

"While he was up on the roof waiting for you, I managed to escape." She presses herself against me and speaks into my ear. I'm assaulted by the lush scent of her hair, the warmth radiating from her body. I put my arms around her.

"Then what?"

"Then I thought about leaving, but I knew you'd come back for me."

"You did?" I feel a surge of affection for her.

There's another shot from inside the warehouse, followed by a shout of helpless anger. Wheels must be shooting at phantoms now.

"I went looking for a weapon," Melanie says. "I found this room, which is where they were keeping my bow and arrow, and a few other things.

"What?"

"I'll show you."

She ignites another match and brings it to a table a few feet away, where she lights a candle. She blows out the match and steps aside. I can only stare in open-mouthed wonder as I approach the table. Her bow and quiver lie at the far end, but the end closest to us is covered in drugs—not pill bottles but packaged marijuana, cocaine, and others, all wrapped and ready to go.

"I think they were drug dealers before the Outbreak," Melanie says, flinching as an unusually aggressive infected throws its entire weight against the door. It'll hold for a while, but not long.

I look around the room. The shelves are packed with even more bricks and packets. The bundles of weed, wrapped in transparent plastic, look brown and dry inside their shells. Some of the shelves contain shoeboxes with the covers removed, exposing neat rows of tiny glass bottles—the kind you stick a needle into to extract the fluid inside.

Wheels fires another shot, and I hear him yell, "Get out here now," followed by, "Oh, *fuck*!"

"I shot him with an arrow right after he lit those fireworks," Melanie tells me. "I laced it with this just in case it only nicked him."

She takes a bottle off a nearby shelf and shows it to me. It's about the size of a shot glass, a quarter full of a transparent liquid I can only identify by reading the label.

"Lysergic acid die..." I don't finish. "It's LSD."

"How do you know?"

"Chemistry class."

"Mr. Rothschild?" When I nod, she says, "What does it do exactly?"

I shrug and put down the bottle. "It makes you trip."

"Like, hallucinations?"

"I think so. I remember him saying it could cause paranoia. How much did you use on that arrow?"

"I soaked the whole tip."

"Good."

We both go silent. I don't hear a peep from Wheels.

"He's stalking us," Melanie says. "We need to get out of here and go someplace safe."

"Not outside. The infected aren't going anywhere. Not without a meal."

"Oh God. My mom and my sister must be freaking out. I can't die here. I need to go home."

Her eyes glisten with fresh tears that catch the candlelight. One slides down her dirty cheek. I wipe it away with my gloved thumb, which reminds me of holding my father's severed head. I can still feel the sticky blood inside my gloves.

"I won't let you die," I tell her. "I promise."

She nods and looks down at her bow and arrow on the table.

"We have to kill him," she says.

I pull the 9mm out of my chest holster.

"I'll do it," I say.

Melanie is about to speak when a loud burst goes off in the building's main storage area. It almost sounds like the grenade I used to kill the Colonel.

Only it's much worse than a grenade. I recognize the sound, and it tells me that Wheels has ditched the hunting rifle.

Now he's using a shotgun.

13

"Come out, come out," Wheels says, his voice muffled by the wall between us. "I'm gonna find you and your little bitch."

I've blown out the candle. The room is pitch black again. I stand by the door and listen. The fact that I can hear his voice over the incessant pounding of the infected means he's close. The windows that look out into the storage area have been boarded up, but a sliver between two of the boards lets me see stacks on the other side, silhouetted against the glow of lanterns he has set up.

I'm thankful for all the noise the infected are making. It's more than enough to mask any sounds I might make opening the door. I don't have my gun anymore, so I'll have to use the spare hunting knife from the emergency pack, then stealth to gain the advantage.

My hand is already on the doorknob when Melanie speaks.

"I'll go with you."

I hesitate. We had agreed that she would stay here with

the 9mm. If Wheels is wearing body armor, the bow and arrow won't do her much good.

I look back, though I can't see her in the dark. Occasionally a pinprick of light appears in the door's viewing hole as the infected move past it.

"I really think you should take the gun," Melanie says. "You can't go out there with just a knife."

"You keep it. Stay here and wait for me, and if I'm not back in ten minutes..."

"I know," she says.

Every muscle in my body tightens with the urge to hold her again. My nose still holds the scent of her hair.

"Melanie," I say.

I can't find the words to express what I feel. She finds them for me.

"Kip, come back to me."

"I will."

I turn the knob, open the door just enough to slide through, and shut it again as quietly as I can. Immediately I fall into a crouch and study my surroundings. The stacks at this end are arranged in a more grid-like fashion, creating aisles of space.

I sneak through them, listening for my enemy. But Wheels has gone dark again. He might be crouched in one of the aisles, waiting for me. Overhead, a suspended metal walkway bends around the storage area, hugging the walls.

No, he wouldn't be up there. Not if he's using a shotgun. A weapon like that is more effective at close range.

I glance into the empty aisles as I creep through the main storage area. Despite the additional lanterns scattered throughout, it's too dark to see much of anything. Armed only with a knife, I keep to the outer aisle in hopes I'll come up behind him.

A blast shatters my train of thought and sends me ducking toward the center. The hunting knife has slipped out of my hand. I'm completely unarmed now.

At the sound of a footstep, I hook around a stack as another blast tears through the space where I had been standing. The pellets make a ringing noise against the metal shelves. I drop to avoid ricochets.

I scramble on knees and elbows to find better cover. The clapping of boots tells me Wheels is running after me. Either he knows I'm not armed—it suddenly hits me how brash I was to part with the 9mm—or he simply doesn't care.

"Where are you, Kip?" he croons into the darkness, and I hear something clicking. "Come out, come out."

The clicking must be coming from the shotgun. He's loading it. A heavier click tells me he has just snapped the barrel back into place.

I'm not an expert in shotguns since my father hated them and collected rifles and pistols instead, but I know enough from my own research to have an idea of what he's carrying. I'm pretty sure it's a double-barreled shotgun. If so, he has to load it after every two shots.

I can't make that assumption without evidence, though. If it's actually a pump-action shotgun, he might have as many as eight rounds at his disposal before he has to reload again.

The space is more open near the storage area's center, the stacks fewer and farther apart. I feel around for something I can throw across the room to distract him. On a shelf above my head is a pair of paint buckets. I nudge one ever so slightly, but it's either full of paint or stuck to the shelf. One next to it feels empty.

I hear a footstep nearby, then another. Does he realize he's being this loud?

The empty can comes off the shelf easily. I hold it in one hand while, with the other, I struggle to unstick the heavier one without making a sound.

I fail at that task. The dried paint around the base makes a ripping sound as the can comes off.

Boots scrape the floor as Wheels runs toward me.

I toss the empty paint can to my left. It lands somewhere with a hollow clatter. He immediately shoots at it—a boom like the entire warehouse caving in, followed by more ringing of lead against the shelves.

I maneuver around the nearest stack, taking the heavier paint can with me. His careless shot has just confirmed his location.

There he is, back turned to me. He's only a silhouette against the dim lamplight.

I swing the paint can as he turns to aim at me. His head is just a black lump above his raised shoulders, but my aim is accurate. I feel the impact a split second before the shotgun coughs out another ear-shattering burst, its muzzle flash lighting the darkness.

"Fuck," he roars.

The can, heavy as it is, definitely hurt him. He isn't down for the count, though. Not even close. He whips around to face me. By now, I'm on the floor, having thrown myself backward to avoid the blast.

His shoulders rise as he takes aim.

The word *shit* tears through my mind, accompanied by the body-length chill that comes from anticipating a world of hurt.

Except there is only a click.

The shotgun went off twice, meaning he has to reload.

I never give him the chance. I'm up in a flash, every muscle in my body tight with the excitement that comes from being alive after tasting certain death.

My first move is a head-butt. As I'm thrusting my forehead toward his nose, I catch a glimpse of the shotgun's barrel and realize I've made a terrible mistake. He's holding the weapon parallel to his chest. With a powerful push, he slams it against my collarbones before my forehead can connect.

I'm thrown off balance and stagger back. As I reach to grab hold of a shelf, he lands a kick against my stomach that knocks me down.

The remaining air goes out of my lungs as Wheels drops all his weight onto me. Straddling my chest, he lifts the shotgun above his head and drives it down toward my face.

I deflect it using both arms, almost fracturing a bone or two.

Ignoring the pain, I drive my right fist into his side, going for the lowest ribs. My knuckles hit a hard, padded surface instead.

Body armor.

"Fuckin' amateur," Wheels says.

He slaps me hard enough to throw stars across my vision.

I cross my arms over my face, no clue what to do next. I'm certain he'll hit me again.

He doesn't. Instead, he pulls my arms apart and lowers his head over mine.

"I'm ex-Navy Seal, kid," he says. "You don't have a chan—"

Before he can finish, I whip my head toward the dark mass of his face. This time, the head butt lands like it should, and I'm treated to the painless impact of solid bone smashing into something soft—his nose, probably.

He swings at me and hits me in the face. Four knuckles crash into my cheekbone. My eyes roll, and I smell blood—his or mine, I can't tell. Despite the pain, I react instantly. Pausing would only give him time to plan his next move.

His ear. That's what I go for when I slap my flattened palm against the side of his head. It lands about how I want it to, enough to stun him long enough for me to grab his body armor, swing my legs, and roll him off.

As we scramble to get away from each other, Wheels suddenly ducks low to the ground. He charges toward me so fast, I barely have time to prepare for a tackle.

Barely. I drop all my weight on my left heel and spin away from him, narrowly missing his charging shoulder. Whirling around to face him, I drop into a defensive stance in case he tries another one.

His dark shape hunkers in front of me. He's bent over now, fumbling with something on the floor.

A hollow scrape of metal against concrete tells me he has picked up the shotgun. By the time he lifts it past his waist, I'm no longer standing in that spot. I'm swinging myself around the nearest stack to put something—anything—between us.

He hasn't reloaded yet, so I imagine he plans to use the shotgun as a club. With the stack between us, I'm protected. Now, though, I've given him all the time in the world to reload.

"Where'd you go, kid," he says in a raspy voice, and I hear the snap of the shotgun being cracked open, followed by the click of a shell being slipped inside.

An idea strikes me. How heavy are these shelves, anyway?

Wheels speaks again. I think he says, "Time to..." though time to what, exactly, I'll never know. Time to die, probably.

And maybe he's right—but not yet.

I heave with all of my strength and manage to tip the shelf over on top of Wheels.

He dives out from under it but doesn't make it all the way.

The shelf lands with a bang so loud I barely hear the shriek of agony from Wheels. Then there is silence, which is even more startling. The infected have momentarily stopped their wall bashing. I imagine them standing out there, gaping stupidly at the inch of space in front of their faces, trying to figure out what the noise was.

They give up, apparently, because the pounding resumes a moment later.

I walk around the toppled stack to find Wheels lying on his stomach. The shotgun is on the floor by his hand, and I kick it away before he can grab it. He lashes out to grab my boot and misses. I step back in case he has any other surprises. Already, I'm wondering how to finish this.

Could I really kill him? A helpless man with no weapon?

"You fucking pussy," Wheels says, grunting and squirming beneath the weight crushing his legs below the knees. "They're gonna tear you and your little girlfriend apart, piece by fucking piece."

"You were a Navy Seal?" I ask him, not sure why I do.

"You bet I was. A little pussy like you has no idea what that means and never will. So go ahead, fucking kill me. I don't care."

"You were never a Seal," I say. "I'm going to forget you ever said that."

Wheels makes a violent *fff* sound that I imagine is the beginning of a curse directed at me.

My boot never gives him the chance. I kick him in the face, hard enough to turn his head a full ninety degrees in the other direction. I don't stop there. Incapable now of controlling the rage sizzling through my nervous system, I kick and stomp with the mindless fury of an infected until, eventually, my boot lands in what feels like a soupy mess.

The rage subsides, and I question whether or not I'll feel something later, some kind of shameful acknowledgment of what I've just done.

Probably not. Things are different now, and I vaguely understand what my father went through in the warzones of the Middle East, where killing an enemy soldier never really hit you on an emotional level. The way he explained it, your mind found ways to justify it, to make the enemy seem less human, so you wouldn't feel bad about killing.

Regardless of how I might deal with it, Wheels deserved to die.

I don't stick around. I scream out Melanie's name, but there's no way she can hear me above the bashing of infected fists against the warehouse walls. I grab the lantern and make my way to the office.

She's in there, but her back is turned to me as she busies herself with aiming the 9mm at the door. The warped lines of light around the curved edges tell me the infected are close to breaking it off the hinges. Another minute, and they'll be inside.

"Melanie," I shout.

She still can't hear me. All of her concentration is on the pistol and the act of keeping it leveled at the door.

I tap her shoulder. She whips around, and I duck at the sudden threat of a gun barrel leveled at my face. When no shot is fired, I rise slowly with my hands up.

"Kip," she says, and I can hear the relief in her voice above the commotion. "Take it."

She passes me the 9mm, then goes after her bow and quiver. I'm not sure how much good either weapon will do against the horde.

"Follow me," I tell her, grabbing a lantern.

We leave the office and I pass her the lantern so I can lock the door we have just shut behind us. Luckily for me, the Colonel (or his predecessor) was paranoid about fortifying every door on the inside as well as the outside. This one uses a steel beam that can slide horizontally through metal fixtures. Better than a simple deadbolt.

Still not enough.

The infected burst into the room I have just sealed and go straight for the next door in their path. The rattling sound it makes tells me the inner door won't hold, either, and for a moment, I'm paralyzed, no idea what to do next.

"The shelves," Melanie says. "Can we use them?"

"Let's try."

She tosses her bow aside where she can reach it later. I holster the pistol and take the lantern from her, putting it on a shelf to maximize our light.

It's incredibly taxing work, even with two of us to share the burden. Tipping the stack onto one side is easy, but the structure is incredibly heavy and tough to drag. When we finally get it propped against the door, I feel a surge of hope.

"Another one," Melanie says.

We run to another that looks empty. We hear glass shatter as the infected realize there's a window with only a layer of wooden boards covering it on the other side. They've begun to slam their fists against the boards, a better option than the door. Fortunately, whoever put up those boards did a damned good job of it. Still, they won't hold forever.

We drag another shelf to the window, count to three, and heave it up high enough to prop it against the topmost board. The lowest one breaks. Diseased hands shoot through it like freakish weeds. They find the shelves and push, sliding the stack an inch across the floor.

Melanie and I look at each other. No need to say what we're thinking.

We drag over another stack and drop it just right so it lies against the bottom edges of the first two. We lucked out in making the original stacks level with each other. Now the three of them form a blocky Y shape that covers the windows and the door, with reinforcement against the floor.

Now what?

Melanie and I throw another glance at each other.

"The walkway," she says and jabs a finger up at the ceiling in case I can't hear her. We're both shouting over the commotion. "There's a catch!"

"A what?" I shout back.

"A *hatch*," she says, cupping her mouth with one hand. "To the roof! Outside!"

It makes sense. The previous residents constructed a hatch to get out onto the rooftop, which is how Wheels was able to shoot at me.

I'm puzzled as to why we might want to go up there. Obviously, it'll get us away from the infected, who would have serious trouble climbing after us, but then what?

An idea takes hold of me. A ridiculously risky one, but it's all I've got.

"We can use his body," I tell her.

She squints at me.

"Wheels! His body!"

She nods, understanding. I swing the lantern toward the spot where I left Wheels. The infected want meat. That's all they care about. And I've just killed the thing they wish to eat most.

"We'll throw him off the roof," I shout at her. "Distract them! Then climb over the other side!"

We make our way toward the corpse. I lead us through the space where I first woke up tied to that torture table. The metal instruments are still there, untouched. The phrase *Pain is just a signal* run through my mind. My only reason for revisiting this particular spot is to grab my utility belt, which lies on the floor at the base of a shelf.

It is still thick with supplies. The Colonel and his friends obviously went through it, removing the ammo and water bottle, but leaving the clamshell mirror and a few other helpful items.

Strapping it around my waist, we find our way to Wheels's body. Removing the toppled stack pinning his legs is simple enough—we count to three, then lift and slide— but carrying him is awkward and slow. We settle on dragging him across the warehouse toward metal stairs that zigzag up to the suspended walkway.

Now we have a real problem. The narrowness of the stairs makes carrying the body more difficult than moving the stacks had been. Especially with one of my hands holding the lantern and my bulky pack constantly bumping the handrails.

Melanie slings her bow over one shoulder so the string crosses her chest. But even with both of her hands free and a smaller pack, her burden is no easier to bear. She hasn't eaten since the last time she and I shared a meal, which was yesterday. The hooded look in her eyes makes me wish I had saved one of the amphetamine pills for her.

Despite her fatigue, she comes up with the idea of taking the lantern away from me, sprinting up the stairs, and resting it on the edge of the walkway. Yellow light washes over her as she makes her way back down.

We get to work carrying Wheels, but it is still extremely awkward and slow. Melanie takes the lead, facing forward with her arms carrying his legs. I'm behind her with Wheels's demolished head resting against my sternum, my hands pushing up against his shoulder blades to keep him aloft.

We make it up the stairs and to the end of the walkway, heaving and panting, before finally dropping the corpse. This is the right spot. I know because a section of the handrail closest to the wall has been cut away, and a makeshift wooden platform leads from the walkway up to the sloped ceiling.

The hatch is visible as three edges are lit by sunlight, the fourth dark from the hinges connecting it to the rest of the roof. Even in the weak glow of the dying lantern, I can tell that a lot of care went into building all of this. So much thought went into it, in fact, that there are even ropes suspended from above on either side of the platform to grab for stability.

I set down the lantern since I won't need it anymore. The platform is about ten feet long and slanted maybe twenty degrees upward. Stable, but we won't know for sure until one of us tests it.

"I'll go first," I say.

Melanie nods. Her drowsy expression almost makes her look apathetic, like it doesn't matter what we do anymore. But as I'm about to turn away, she grabs my hand, turns me around to face her, and plants a quick kiss on my lips.

"Be careful, Kip."

"You too."

My heart drums against my ribs as I make my way along the platform, gripping the side ropes to steady myself. I imagine each shaky step being my last before the entire thing collapses. At the other end, I lift the hatch a few inches, glad it isn't locked, and briefly take note of features like hinges, a locking mechanism, and even a rope you can use to pull it shut from inside.

I throw it open. A sudden wash of steely light leaves me blind for a moment. When I can see again, I look at Melanie. She has tilted her head back and is smiling sadly up at the light. In her mind, it must symbolize freedom. She has, after all, been trapped in here with a murdering cannibal all night.

I make my way back down the platform to grab hold of Wheels's boots, having to endure the foul stench of them. Can't be much worse than the crushed head Melanie has to stare at. By the time we move him to the other end of the suspended platform, the stacks we set up below finally slide away and land flat with a bang.

The infected burst through the windows and the door with newfound ease, as if their rage at having been trapped this long has doubled their strength. The warehouse fills with their ravenous clamoring.

"They're inside," I say, more to speed us along than anything else. It's clear by a sudden widening of her eyes that Melanie is well aware of the situation.

"You need to climb outside first," she says.

We drop the corpse. I pull myself through the hatch, with a helpful push from her. The platform shakes wildly now from all the extra movement. How many people was this thing designed to hold? Definitely not more than two, which means I need to get Wheels off immediately.

I'm outside now. The space around me is suddenly vast and quiet and full of light. It's as if I've entered a completely different world. The quiet tells me the infected have all entered the warehouse.

I reach through the hatch, stretching my left arm as far as it will go, my other hand clutching the edge for support. From this angle, the task ahead of us seems impossible.

There is no way this is going to work.

Melanie can't lift the body alone. Even if she could do it, my arm muscles are spent; there is no way I will be able to raise it and help her out afterward. And to attempt it all with one arm, the other occupied with keeping me in place...

It gets worse.

The whole point in bringing Wheels with us was to throw his corpse to the infected *outside*, giving them something to focus on while we made our escape over the opposite edge. But the infected are no longer out here. They're *inside* the warehouse now, meaning our idea is worthless.

It also means I don't need to lift the corpse.

"Melanie, let go of him!" I scream at her. "Grab my hand!"

"What?" she shouts back at me.

She is bent beneath the corpse's weight, struggling to drape the legs over her shoulders and hold the ankles.

"It won't work," I tell her. "Leave him there! Take my hand! You have to get out!"

"I don't understand, Kip!"

A grinding *pop* goes off next to me. The extra weight on the platform has yanked out one of the metal loops screwed into the ceiling—a fixture installed for the sake of attaching a support rope. Melanie ducks as the platform drops a few inches. She blinks up at me, more confused than afraid. It hasn't hit her yet that she is going to die.

"Take my hand! Melanie, just do it!"

Directly below her, the infected have gathered into a ravenous mob. The knowledge of what is about to happen sinks in, and Melanie lets out a sob.

"Oh, no. Kip!"

"Grab my hand," I shout at her. "Now! You have to jump!"

She shakes her head at me, eyes glistening with tears. Her face is so close I could reach down and touch her. But only if release my other hand.

There is another pop as a second metal loop detaches from the ceiling. The support rope attached to it falls. I reach my arms through the opening toward her, and Melanie jumps at exactly the right moment. My hands find one of her arms, and I grab her as the platform detaches completely and sails down, along with Wheels's corpse, into the mob.

I press my forehead to the roof's metal surface, pulling with my neck and arm muscles and every other muscle to get one of her arms out of the hole. Then I roll away, bringing her arm with me, never letting go even as it bends and scrapes along the edge.

There is no moment, like in the movies, where the hero gracefully pulls the damsel through to safety. Instead, she and I are locked in a brutal, messy struggle in which victory is measured one inch at a time, one painful scream after another. Her arm might as well be a stubborn weed I'm trying to yank out of a garden, with the merciless way I'm pulling on it.

When she's finally through, I slam the lid over the opening. The arm that saved her life dangles limply at her side. She almost faints, and I grab her before she can roll down the sloping surface.

The arm is out of its socket. Though I've never actually done it, I manage to pop it back in after instructing Melanie to cover her mouth with her other hand to stifle a scream.

She doesn't scream—not even a squeak—as I slam it back into place.

Instead, she rolls away, clutching the shoulder and squirming from the pain. When she finally sits back up, the first thing she does is slap me across the face. I reel, covering the sore spot with one hand.

"Do it again," I tell her.

I leave my cheek exposed.

She surprises me by grabbing my neck and pulling me in for a hungry kiss. I hold her in a fierce embrace that makes her whimper a bit from the pain still in her shoulder.

I could die right here, content. But Melanie kills that peaceful moment.

"The virals," she says.

They are still gathered in the storage space below us, lifting a noise that makes the roof vibrate. A whole horde of them. I glance over the rooftop and into the back parking lot where I had entered earlier.

The lot is mostly empty. I see only a few stragglers, the blind ones trying to feel their way around. One missing both legs drags itself forward. None of them poses much of a threat.

"They're all inside the warehouse," I say.

"No," Melanie says, still dazed. "Leaving. They're—they're coming out again…"

"How do you know?"

"I saw them. They know we're not inside. They're coming."

I scramble over to the hatch and hold it open. My eyes take a few seconds to adjust to the darkness, but eventually I see that Melanie is right. The horde of infected—finished with devouring Wheels's corpse—is now pushing outward, trying to funnel through the door they used to get inside.

The scent of gasoline wafts up to me.

"Can we jump down from here?" Melanie says.

I shake my head. "No way."

We're two stories up. If we were to jump from here to the pavement, our chances of breaking an ankle or a leg would be astronomically high.

"The grappling rope," I say. "It's our only chance."

I swing off my pack, locate the grappler, and yank out all twelve feet of rope.

"Here." I hand it to Melanie. "Fix it to the edge. Climb down."

"But what are you—"

I ignore her for the time being and focus on digging through my pack, seized by a burning idea.

When I find what I need, I hold it up in a firm grip and shoot a warning look at Melanie. Her eyes widen at the sight of it.

"Go," I tell her.

She turns and makes for the edge. Within seconds, she finds a rust-eaten patch in the corrugated surface and sets the grappler into place.

We lock eyes—a solemn, hopeful gaze—as Melanie slips over the edge and disappears.

I give her thirty seconds, time I spend studying the shifting mass of infected through the hatch. They're like a bunch of partygoers in a crowded nightclub that has suddenly caught fire, so desperate to get out that they can't help but climb over each other, effectively clogging the only escape route.

At the center of the storage area is the Colonel's enormous stash of gasoline cans. The infected jostle the shelves, knocking the cans over, and I can only hope some of the gas has leaked out to pool around their feet. The intensified smell tells me it might have already happened.

The grenade feels heavy as I hold it over the opening. I'm at twenty-six seconds in the countdown, on my way to thirty—and destruction.

Twenty-seven...

Twenty-eight...

Twenty-nine...

Thirty.

"Good-bye," I whisper.

I pull the pin and fling the grenade—a fragger like the one I used to kill the Colonel and Bandanna—into the warehouse. It lands nowhere near the gas cans, but that shouldn't matter in such a closed space.

Five seconds. That's all I have until the boom.

I sprint toward the grappler, gather a few feet of rope, and hold on for dear life as I throw myself over the edge, hoping the grappler will hold.

It does, but only for a second as a violent tremor jostles the building, accompanied by a skull-cracking boom. The blast rips apart the boarded window in front of me and sends a shower of splinters into my body, and my ears fill with a steady, high-pitched whistle that drowns out every other noise.

That whistle is all I hear as I fall two stories toward concrete.

14

I'm only half-conscious when I feel something soft break my fall.

Not *soft*, exactly, but it certainly isn't concrete. It isn't my pack, either, since I no longer feel it around my back. My eyes sting too much to open them, but I know—I'm *certain*, actually—that I've landed on top of Melanie. She must have tried to break my fall.

Reality becomes a dark, throbbing mess of sensations I can't decipher. My eyes won't open. The whistle in my ears mixes with a scream I know is mine, though I can't feel my mouth.

Something grabs my coverall and drags me away from the building.

Hands. I know from the way the nails dig into me.

All I can think is the infected are taking me away from the smoke; away from Melanie, who might still be alive; away from this unfinished life so they can devour what's left of it.

"Kip!"

She's alive.

I open my eyes—the left one, anyway—and blink away dust. My right eye remains sealed and stings inside its socket.

Steeped in shock and disbelief, I reach up to touch it.

"Don't," Melanie says, pushing down my hand. "Can you feel your legs?"

I move them, surprised there is no pain. But that's because all of the pain is concentrated in my lower back.

With Melanie's help, I get up, like an old man recovering from a bad spill. The pain in my lower back is awesome—and I mean that in the literal sense, as in "something that inspires awe." Never have I felt pain like this in my life, nor did I know it existed.

With a sharp cry, my legs give out and I tumble back to the ground.

"Oh God," Melanie says, bending over me. "What is it? How does it feel?"

"Hurting," is all I can say between gasps.

"More of them are going to come. Let's try and make it to the trees. You can do it."

No way in hell, I want to tell her. But I'm gasping too hard to speak. The pain is like having spears driven into me, bypassing my skin but shredding the muscle and bone beneath.

"Go," I tell her through clenched teeth. "Run..."

"I won't leave you."

"Go!"

"But I love you, Kip."

Finally the pain is too much, and I pass out.

When I open my left eye again, I see high grass and trees. My nose rakes in a smell of weeds, dry and untamed, and the more powerful, acrid stench of smoke. I'm lying on my left side, my face against fabric Melanie must have laid out for me.

She appears in my field of vision and crouches next to me.

"How do you feel?"

The pain in my back is still there, though now it's more of a dull throb than the vicious, stabbing, ripping, grinding agony from before.

"How long have I been out?" I ask her.

"Ten minutes." She smiles at me. "The longest ten minutes of my life."

Over the new few minutes, I manage to stand, sling my pack over my shoulders, and take a few steps without too much grunting. The fact that I can stand and walk means I haven't broken my back, though running right now would be impossible.

"All right," I say, "let's g—"

The pain flares up suddenly, the same vicious, stabbing, ripping, grinding...

"Oh God fucking damn it," I say as my legs give out again.

I fall to my knees and struggle to remain upright, as if doing so is a way of resisting the truth: that this is the end of my road, right here. Once I collapse, there will be no getting up again.

One thing I need to do first, before the end.

"Run home," I tell Melanie. "Don't argue. Just go."

I sound like my father in his final moments: defeated, faced with certain death, and ready for it.

Melanie falls to her knees in front of me, adoring green eyes roaming my face.

"I'll wait," she says. "You just need more time. The smoke will keep away the virals for—"

I cut her off. "Shut up."

A wounded look comes over her. "I'm sorry, Kip."

I fight back a surge of self-pity. When she's gone, I'll let myself cry.

"There's something you should know," I tell her. "I don't love you. I was going to hurt you. Rape you. And kill your mother and sister so I could take your stash. I've done it before."

"You're lying," she says with a few quick shakes of her head.

"I'm not. It's the truth. So get out of here."

Her eyes fill with tears. She is still shaking her head—more slowly now, as if in addition to shock and sadness, she also feels disappointment. My face remains as hard as I can make it. The constant sting and throb in my gouged right eye makes it easier to feel like a monster, like Wheels, whose spirit I pretend has possessed me.

"Kip..."

"I said shut up. Don't you get it? I would've followed you home to your stash. That's all I cared about. I don't feel anything for you. Just go away so I can die in peace."

The words ring hollow in my ears. My heart shivers instead of beats, pumping ice-cold blood that chills the rest of me. That same chill washes over Melanie. I can tell by the way her eyes widen slightly in disbelief.

"Go away," I tell her. "This is your fault."

"Is it?" she says with a sniffle. "Then just tell me one thing."

"Aren't you listening to me?" I yell at her. "Just go! Fucking get out of here!"

She blinks but doesn't budge an inch.

"That's all I needed to know," she says.

"What are you talking about?"

My entire body is trembling now, my back painfully stiff. Another minute and I'll be on the ground again. She can't be here when that happens. She might never leave.

"What are you talking about?" I ask her again. "Why won't you just leave me here?"

"Because," she says, blinking away fresh tears, "you truly love me."

Before I can say anything, she leans forward and kisses me.

My resolve vanishes. I don't want to die, I just want to be with her. My body conveys the message by trembling all the more fiercely. After a moment, our lips part, but our foreheads remain pressed against each other as we both start crying. I place a hand on the side of her face and caress it.

"I'm sorry," I whisper to her. "I didn't mean it."

"I know that. You're a bad liar, Kip. That's why I love you."

I want to respond, but I wilt at a sudden onslaught of pain. She catches me and lowers me to the ground.

"Your eye," she says. "I'll take care of it. Just breathe, let your muscles relax."

She goes for her pack and digs out a handkerchief and a tube of anti-bacterial ointment. She spreads the ointment over the handkerchief and gets to work wrapping it around my head to cover my right eye.

But what for? It's over for me. Doesn't she understand that?

"Get up," she says.

"No," I tell her.

My voice is soft and calm. There's no use arguing. I silently tell my father that I know exactly how he felt when I went for that medicine. Why bother?

"Please," Melanie says, her eyes pleading. "Don't give up."

"I'm—done," I manage to say.

She throws herself over me.

"I don't want you to die. I don't want to be without you."

I push her away and look down at my chest.

"The gun," I say.

Sobbing uncontrollably now, Melanie nods and says, "Okay."

She pulls the 9mm out of my chest holster and stands over me. I raise a hand to pause her for a second as I push myself up to my knees. A sharp ache and a spell of dizziness nearly force me back down, but I hold steady and look at her, shivering.

"Pull the slide," I tell her. "Don't be scared."

"Are you sure?"

I nod gravely at her. "I'll slow you down."

"No you won't. I can—"

"Stop. This is how it is."

Melanie nods again before yanking back the slide.

"I'm sorry. I'm so, so sorry."

"It's okay. I'm luckier than anyone."

"I'm glad I met you. I'll never forget you. And—and I love you."

My heart breaks. I look down at the weeds and close my eyes against a surge of hot tears.

"I love you too," I tell her.

15

Melanie never fires.

Instead of a gunshot, I hear the low rumble of an engine.

My left eye shoots open. I look up at Melanie, feeling like I've awoken out of a nightmare. She swings the pistol in the direction of the warehouse. I twist to see what might be there and my back gives out again. I fall to my stomach, gritting my teeth in anger.

"What is that?" she says.

"I don't know," I say between grunts. "But get down."

She drops to one knee. The engine noise grows louder. It's coming from farther up the road that leads out of the industrial park—a battered truck engine, it sounds like. My uncle Frank had an old pickup that made a noise just like it.

"It's a truck," I say. "I'm almost sure of it."

The rumbling dies down until it cuts off completely, followed by the thin squeal of brakes as the vehicle comes to a full stop.

I can barely see anything. From down here, my view is blocked by a tangled mess of brambles between me and the parking lot. Crouching would solve the problem, but my back screams at me to stay put.

"Can you see anything?" I ask Melanie.

She rises into a crouch and gazes out at the lot.

"No, nothing at all. Not even virals."

I let out an impatient sigh. Who knows what it could mean for us? The people in that truck could be killers or saviors.

I crane my neck to get a better view, but all I see is the black smoke billowing out of the warehouse's busted upper windows. A plume of it escapes the hatch to form a dull smear across the sky. The building is still standing, but it looks oddly bent; I doubt it'll be standing a month from now.

If I extend my neck a few more inches, I can look through a narrow slit in the brambles that allows for a limited view of the building's far corner and a slice of the parking lot. Several seconds go by in which I don't see or hear anything out of the ordinary, until finally something appears.

An infected man comes stumbling around the corner wearing a coat of flames, arms swinging around his smoking torso like he's trying to clear the air of insects. A normal person would have dropped to the ground and rolled. Not this guy; obviously confused, he makes a series of irrational and erratic motions, like he's stone drunk instead of on fire.

Seconds go by. How is it that he doesn't fall?

A rifle goes off. Melanie and I shudder at the sound.

Still covered in flames, the infected man lunges as if an invisible leash around his neck has been yanked. He falls flat on his face in a burst of smoke.

"Raiders," I say. "But why—"

Melanie cuts me off. "Kip, I'm going to carry you. Let's go."

"No, wait."

I can't turn away just yet. There is still a mystery to solve.

What kind of raider would waste ammo on an infected person already on the verge of death? And why would they stick around when it's obvious only a miracle could have saved any supplies that might have been inside the warehouse?

Unless the good guys have arrived, and shooting the flaming man was a mercy kill.

"I need to see who it is," I tell her.

The next minute is torture. Who's around that corner? Why are they taking so long to appear? Maybe they're trying the side door, but that doesn't make sense. The inside is clearly destroyed. All they can expect to find in there is smoke and debris.

"What if it's raiders?" Melanie says. "A whole truck full of them?"

"The truck," I say. "We might be able to take it."

"You mean kill them? With the condition you're in?"

The engine starts again with a rumble.

"Shhh..." I motion for her to get down.

Through the narrow slit in the brambles, I watch as something big appears from around the corner. It inches slowly into the lot. Even though all I see are isolated details —a curved metal plate, a muddy headlight, a side mirror above a dent in the door—I know enough to confirm my fear. The vehicle is a battered, dust-covered truck with a snowplow attached to the front, and it's about to drive right over the corpse of the infected man.

I flinch at the sound of bones crunching beneath the wheels.

"Oh my God," Melanie whispers.

My neck cramps up. I lower my head and slip out the clamshell mirror. I snap it open with one hand and lift it to catch a glimpse of the parking lot.

I'm just in time. As the truck crawls into view, I see a dark, hunched figure in the driver's seat, a passenger's seat that is thankfully empty, and a burly black man standing in the back. He leans against the roof and holds a hunting rifle.

My initial thought is that I'm looking at raiders, but that assessment quickly changes when I see the cargo being transported in the truck's bed.

People are sitting against the sides, heads bowed in misery. They look to be all female, but as I twist the mirror to follow their movement, I catch sight of a man's graying head.

Suddenly, Melanie grabs my arm and pulls it down.

"They might see the reflection of your mirror," she says.

"Good call."

I ponder what their arrival means. Unlike raiders, these men didn't come here to gather supplies. If that were the case, they would have taken off by now, uninterested in a fiery wreck. These men in the truck are seeking something else.

Melanie stares at my face. I slide the mirror into its pouch, avoiding her questioning look. The last thing I want is for her to panic.

"What did you see?" she asks me.

"Melanie, whatever happens, you stay down. Promise me."

"Kip, who are they?"

I hesitate. "Slavers."

Her face crumples in a look of terror. "Oh, Jesus. Oh my God."

"Shhh... Just stay down."

"But they know someone is here. The smoke..."

I know what she's thinking. Someone had to light the warehouse on fire, after all.

There might still be hope, though.

"Not if they think the fire killed them," I say. "If they think everyone was inside, they'll go in, or leave."

Melanie finds no relief in my words. She looks away, shaking her head slowly. I want to put a hand on her back and tell her they'll be gone soon, but even I don't believe that. Until now, the only thugs we've had to deal with are raiders, who know only three things: how to steal, rape, and kill.

Slavers, on the other hand, are a different breed.

They're like those people that try to build utopias in the mountains, my father explained to me once. *Except they don't recruit doctors or carpenters. They're not interested in rebuilding society or living a long and healthy life. All they care about is satisfying their animal urges while doing the least amount of work possible. The unfortunate souls they take back to their camps become slaves—old men who can work without posing a threat; old women who can plant gardens, cook, and wash their clothes; young girls they keep for pleasure. That, my dear son, is why slavers don't go out on supply runs, because supplies are temporary and finite. But people are the gift that keeps on giving.*

I recall those words—*the gift that keeps on giving*—as I stare at the pistol in Melanie's hands. Should those men find us, they will shoot me on sight, no questions asked. But Melanie they'll keep, feeding off her youth and energy for only God knows how many years or decades.

"We'll kill them," I say. "Give me the gun."

She hands it over.

"You can't shoot them from here, though," she says. "The trees."

I believe her, but I look for a line of sight anyway. My lower back is still a knot of pain and stiffness. Lifting myself into a crouched position is too risky—my back might give out again—but I might have a clear line of sight through a path that lies between us and the back corner of the parking lot, where I can see some of the red tanks.

"Right there," I say, gesturing toward it with a thrust of my chin.

Melanie studies the narrow space.

The truck is still moving. I can tell not just by the quiet rumble of the engine, which could simply be idling, but by the constant, quiet sound of wheels crunching along the pavement. My guess is they plan on turning in a wide, slow arc so the guy with the rifle can scan the surrounding woods from his elevated position.

"I need them to keep driving forward."

"All the way to the back?" Melanie says. "What if they turn around?"

I lift the 9mm just high enough to answer her question. The look she gives me in response tells me she thinks I'm crazy.

We stare at each other, listening to the truck crunching toward the back of the lot. I aim down the length of the path. Maybe I can shoot the driver while he's in the act of turning—assuming he enters my line of sight.

But that isn't going to happen. Melanie places her hand on my arm and gently lowers it.

"What are you doing?" I ask her.

She slips the bow off her shoulders and sets it aside, then reaches back to gather all of her arrows into one hand. She sets those aside as well.

"Melanie, don't move," I tell her in a fierce whisper.

I reach out to grab her, but I end up closing my fingers around empty air. Melanie is already on her feet. Within seconds, she's standing at the edge of the parking lot, in full view if the man standing in the truck turns around—a healthy teenage girl with her hands up in clear surrender, not a weapon in sight, giving herself to a pair of men that might even be worse than the Colonel and his merry band of killers.

I want to shout at her to run, just run away, as fast as she can. But I keep silent. The man with the rifle has spotted her and has her in his sights. He could easily shoot me the moment I make a move. Then Melanie would truly be screwed, as my gun is the only chance she has.

She continues moving along the edge of the parking lot toward the back corner, and I watch as the truck makes a sharp turn and starts driving straight toward Melanie.

This might actually work.

I aim the pistol at the space in front of Melanie. With a roar of its shaky engine, the old Dodge lurches across the lot, coming to a stop almost where I need it to. Ignoring the pain in my back, I crawl on elbows and knees to get a better view, but not far enough to risk exposure.

"Hold it!" a man shouts. "Stop right there!"

Melanie freezes mid-step.

"Don't hurt me," she says, lifting her arms higher.

I crane my neck to see around the tree trunk that's in my way. The black guy with the dreadlocks leans over the truck's roof, aiming his hunting rifle at Melanie. The weapon is dirty, with a worn stock, and his technique is utterly flawed—rather than tilt his head inward to sight along the barrel's length, he tilts it away.

The driver-side door creaks open and slams shut. The

driver appears from around the side of the truck opposite me, taking careful but confident steps toward Melanie as he tucks a shiny revolver into the back of his pants. He's a fleshy, orange-bearded man with a protruding gut and a perfectly bald head. This tells me he's from a camp where shaving—and its inevitable waste of water—is a habit instead of a luxury.

He wears a dark blue, plaid shirt that appears to be clean and is tucked into an equally fresh pair of jeans. His boots are muddy but intact. As he approaches Melanie, he grabs his belt around the sides and lifts his pants in a manly gesture. This is a guy who grooms himself and takes care of his clothes as if the Outbreak never happened—as if survival were not the most urgent matter.

Despite his manly strut, his voice is thin and high, and I detect the uncertainty of a man who never learned to wear his power with the same ease that comes naturally to men like the Colonel. It probably still comes as a surprise to him every time he beds a pretty girl, even against her will. Before the Outbreak, decent women probably ignored him.

I keep the 9mm aimed at him.

"Are you alone?" he asks Melanie.

She nods.

"You know what happened here?"

Another nod, this one more frantic.

"You feel like tellin' me? Or do I have to, uh"—smiling, he throws a glance over his shoulder at the man with the rifle, then looks back at Melanie—"do I have to fuck the truth out of you? Huh, girl?"

His threat falls flat. He must know it did. But who is there to judge him in this new world, where men like him can make their own laws just by pointing a gun?

Hatred wells inside of me. It eats away at the knot in my back, restoring me, letting me to rise into a crouch.

"Just don't hurt me," Melanie says. "I'll tell you anything you want, just please don't hurt me."

"Oh, no worries, no worries," the driver says with a dismissive wave. "I'm not gonna hurt you. I'll treat you real good. A pretty girl like you will have everything she needs. Food, decent clothes, a pot to piss in, a sleeping bag to keep you warm at night. I just want to know what happened here. That's all, sweetheart."

Melanie nods and lets her arms drift down.

"Ho'd on nah, honey," the one with the rifle says, a husky voice. "Don' make me go an' shoot ya."

One of his thick dreadlocks dangles between his face and the rifle. It's right in his line of sight. Melanie lifts her arms again. The one with the plaid shirt motions for his partner to calm down.

"Relax, Johnny. She's just a girl. She ain't a threat to us."

"You check to see if she be packing, Eddie?" Johnny says. "Even dese girls can fight. You know well as I do."

The more Johnny talks, the wider the distance between his head and the rifle becomes. Another dreadlock swings down into his line of sight. At this point, if he had to fire suddenly, he wouldn't hit Melanie if she were a brick wall facing him.

Unless he's an expert who just happens to be full of himself.

My finger grazes the trigger. I could shoot Johnny first, but I'm afraid Eddie could be a quicker shot with that revolver than his casual demeanor implies. And if I shoot Eddie first, Johnny might automatically fire the rifle, hitting Melanie by chance.

"Let me handle this," Eddie says, needlessly pulling up his pants again.

If Eddie goes for his revolver, I will shoot him first. Johnny will most likely swing the rifle in my direction. If he does that, he'll never get the chance to aim it.

Eddie reaches behind his back.

I almost shoot him, but Melanie speaks and Eddie freezes. I give it a few more seconds.

"They tried to take it from me," Melanie says, sounding girlish and desperate.

Eddie's brow furrows in suspicion.

"Take what, sweetheart?"

"The men who made that fire. They tried to take my virginity, but I got away. I made the fire and I got away."

A sob spills out of her. Smiling now, Eddie reaches out in a calming gesture, no longer about to pull the revolver. He approaches Melanie as if to soothe her. Either he genuinely feels pity for her, or the thought of Melanie still being a virgin has excited him to the point of complete idiocy. How does he know she isn't packing a knife?

Now I'm aiming at Johnny. His rifle poses the most immediate threat.

Take out Johnny first, then shoot Eddie in the head before he can whip out his revolver.

"Hey, now," Eddie says to Melanie, taking another step toward her, to which Melanie responds by taking a step back.

I'm about to squeeze the trigger and erase Johnny from the picture when Melanie, in a moment of cleverness, points at the warehouse and shouts, "There they are!"

Johnny swings around with his rifle to aim at his imaginary attackers. Before he can complete the turn, I squeeze the trigger and put a bullet in his skull. The sky goes pink above his head with misted blood.

There are screams from the women in the truck as Johnny falls among them. My pistol, aimed squarely at Eddie's midsection now, makes another loud crack, only a second after the first.

Eddie drops his revolver—I'm actually impressed that he managed to get it out so quickly—and doubles over like a man about to vomit. He lifts his head to get a look at his executioner.

I let him study me, crouched there among the trees with my pistol aimed at him. But I don't shoot. Instead, I watch the realization dawn on Eddie that coming here was the worst mistake of his life. After a few moments during which the color drains from his face, he coughs out a burst of blood and tips over onto the pavement.

He is still alive and conscious. A belly wound is a terrible way to die. He watches me approach, probably wondering why I'm wincing in pain when he's the one who's been shot. But the ache in my back has diminished into a dull throb, and I manage to bend over and pick up the revolver. It goes straight into my utility belt for later inspection. I barely notice Melanie get up and run into the woods where we left our stuff.

"Kill me," Eddie says in a trembling voice.

With a solemn shake of my head, I tell him honestly why I won't.

"I don't want to waste the bullet."

He blinks stupidly at me, and then his eyes crinkle at the corners, promising tears and weeping. I still won't waste a bullet on him. But I also don't want to hear him cry.

As I go for my knife, Melanie takes care of the matter for

me. She puts an arrow into his head. It makes a dull crack as it enters, killing him instantly.

The people in the truck have watched the whole thing. When it's finished, they regard Melanie and me with dumbfounded expressions.

"You're safe," I tell them as I open the tailgate.

Melanie and I drag Johnny's corpse out of the truck and toss it aside. I give the hunting rifle a quick once over and toss that aside as well. Old and poorly maintained. Probably would have jammed on him if he had tried to shoot.

The prisoners seem to trust us, especially the old man. Dressed in a worn black sweater and jeans, he watches me through a squint. A smile rises inside his scraggly white beard. A few of the girls begin to cry openly in what I can tell is pure relief. The old woman extends a hand to Melanie. She receives it warmly and gives it a reassuring grip.

"You're all free," I tell them. "But I recommend you let us take you to a safe place. We have a house not far from here. It's empty, and there's food and water."

They accept this in silence, and I perform a headcount. There are two teenage girls, three women in their twenties and thirties, and the old couple. All of them are frighteningly skinny and dressed in clothes that clearly haven't been changed or washed in over a week.

"Ride with me," I tell Melanie.

She helps me into the truck. I slide over seats covered in greenish fabric riddled with holes. It stinks of body odor in here. A bobblehead doll is stuck to the dash. Its enormous head shivers and shakes, the bright orange swaths of hair above its freckled face and gap-toothed smile clearly that of the "What, me worry?" guy from those old *Mad* magazines.

I tear it off the dash and fling it outside. With a hard turn of the key, I start the engine. It comes to life with a comforting rumble.

"How's your eye?" Melanie says.

"I'll live."

The words *without depth perception* run through my mind but go unsaid.

"And your back?"

I nod. "Better."

Melanie leans over and plants a kiss along my chin, just below the handkerchief she secured there earlier.

"Your house," I say. "Then we'll figure out the rest."

She nods. "Okay."

I drive us onto the main road weaving through the industrial park. Infected stragglers have started to appear from all directions, probably having heard the sound of the gunshots and picked up the scent of the two slavers, but even those capable of running aren't fast enough to catch up. I'm thankful for the plow as we hit a few that stray into our path.

"I hope Mom and Sarah are okay," Melanie says, biting her nails.

"I'm sure they're fine. Do you have any gasoline at your house?"

She looks at me, wide-eyed. "Not anymore. Why?"

"We've got half a tank. Enough to get us there, but I'll have to do a supply run."

She puts a hand on my thigh. "*We'll* have to do a supply run."

We both shudder as a bang goes off behind our heads: the small window in the back opening. I glance at the rear-view mirror. The old man squints back at me.

"Sorry," he says. "Window caught along the darn track."

"It's okay," Melanie says, twisting around to face him. "How is everyone?"

"Much better now, miss."

I keep my eyes on the road. "Need anything?"

"Just a name," the man says. "Pete Hirscham. And you are?"

Melanie and I introduce ourselves. We keep it on a first-name basis since we might have to part ways with these people at some point. At least, that's how I think about it.

"I just wanted to say thank you for saving my family," Pete says.

"Are they your daughters?" Melanie asks him.

He gives a single, firm nod. "And my wife, Linda. My sons Luke, Michael, and Tobias perished during a gathering hunt. We were on our way to a community called Brightrock when we happened upon those two men in the woods. I guess they were trying to take us back to their camp. I'm glad that didn't happen. You youngsters are a gift from the Lord."

The way he said "Lord" tell me he means it literally. His eyes have gathered moisture.

"Brightrock," I say. "Are you sure it's a real place?"

"Oh, yes. I've laid eyes on it myself. My wife and daughters stayed in the woods while I went ahead. It's about the purest place left on Earth. A community devoted to God. It was when I returned that we got kidnapped. I blame myself for it."

I swerve to avoid an overturned car but can't avoid plowing into an infected man crawling on all fours to get across the street.

If there is a God, I thank Him for the snowplow.

"Anyhow, I intend to return," Pete says. "You kids are

welcome to come and bring your families. We could use the extra hands, especially those fit for gathering hunts."

Melanie and I glance at each other. She lifts her brow in uncertainty, mirroring how I feel about such an arrangement.

"I don't want to offend you," I tell the old man, "but we're not really religious—"

"It's all right, son," he says and reaches inside to lay a hand on my shoulder. "I was a pastor at a church north of here. I met many young men like you. When they had questions about the Lord, I preached His word. But when they weren't interested, I told them I loved them anyway, and that I hoped they treated others with the compassion that makes us all kin." His expression darkens. He gives a righteous nod. "Not like those two men back there. They were no kin of mine. Animals is what they were."

"I want to go there," Melanie tells him. "To Brightrock, with my mother and my little sister."

"Hearing that makes my heart sing," Pete says, and I can tell he's genuinely pleased.

We're ten minutes away from Melanie's house, which is a few miles down the road from our high school. I'd rather postpone this conversation until after I've had a meal and decent night's rest.

"You have military training," Pete says. "But you're too young to have served. You were, what, sixteen, seventeen during the Great Reckoning?"

I nod, assuming "the Great Reckoning" is just a biblical-sounding name for "the Outbreak." I like his version better, actually.

"I just turned seventeen when it started to spread," I tell him. "I was never in the military, but my father was."

"And he trained you—trained you *well*, I see."

I nod again, hoping he won't ask me about my Dad.

"Was he in Special Forces?"

"He was. What makes you say that?"

Pete grins. I sense he has something hidden up his sleeve.

It turns out he does. Literally.

"I want to show you something," he says.

He pulls back from the window and takes off his black sweater, evoking a cry of protest from his wife.

"Peter, put that back on," she says in a cutting voice.

The old pastor ignores her and sticks his arm through the window. He's wearing a yellow undershirt that was once white. I watch with growing interest as he lifts the right sleeve to expose a tattoo the runs along his triceps.

"Oh, not that ugly thing," his wife nags at him.

My eyes widen. I can't believe what I'm seeing.

Rendered in what looks like ancient, faded black paint is a dagger with the blade pointing down. Ornamented with jewels and a leather grip, the blade is partially covered by a coiling scroll on which I read three words, one on each coil.

DEATH
BEFORE
DISHONOR

Below the dagger's point is an elaborate logo that reads:

75 RANGER RGT

"My father was a Ranger," I tell him, "and then a Green Beret. Maybe you knew him. Arthur Garrity?"

"Doesn't ring a bell. But he was my brother. You can be

sure of that." He grips my shoulder, then pats it. "And that makes you my kin."

I'm not sure how to respond. "Thank you, Pete."

He smiles and tips his head at Melanie before backing away from the window and into the receiving arms of his wife. She urges him to put on his sweater, and he immediately complies.

Five minutes later, we arrive at Melanie's house, and I follow her instructions to drive onto the grass and pull around the back. It's much nicer than mine, but hidden deep inside a neighborhood where stretches of forest separate each residence, similar to my family's place. Probably why they survived so long without getting attacked.

Melanie runs to the garage door and pounds a distinct beat against it that could never be replicated by accident. It almost sounds like Morse code.

There's a clicking and clanking noise from above—locks and chains being undone. The window above the garage door is boarded up, nails holding it in place, but the way it swings open tells me the nails and boards are just an elaborate disguise.

In the dark opening, two heads rise cautiously to peek over the edge, one blonde, the other auburn-haired. The blonde one is a little girl. Sarah. The other must be Melanie's mom.

They're both cautious enough to hold back squeals and shouts, though the little girl has to clamp both hands over her mouth to contain her excitement. Her mother's face lights up with joy, and immediately she drops a rope ladder through the window and motions for her daughter to climb inside.

I watch with a growing sense of hope as Melanie turns to me, smiling.

"Go," I tell her. "I'll hold the rear for now and help the others."

As I watch her climb gracefully up the front of the garage, I feel a hand settle on my shoulder. Pete is standing next to me, wearing his ratty black sweater again. Only he isn't watching Melanie climb. He's looking up at the clouds.

I expect him to say something God-related, about being blessed or smiled upon by the Lord.

"It's going to rain," he says instead, then turns to help his family out of the truck.

I smile at the simplicity of his words.

"Spoken like a true survivalist," I say.

"Not all men of God live with their heads in the clouds, you know."

"Especially not ones that used to be Rangers."

"Not many of us left, unfortunately."

He slides his hands into his jeans pockets. Together, we watch Melanie slip through the window and pull her mother and sister into a fierce embrace.

"I guess we should help your family," I say, looking at Pete.

I can't tell if he heard me. He's squinting with happiness at his daughters, the youngest of whom—a gangly teenager—is struggling to place a foot on the ladder's bottommost rung with help from her mother.

"Let's do that, son," he says finally.

It takes several minutes to help them up, and on a few occasions, I think I hear the moans of a nearby infected, which makes me pull my gun.

But it's just the wind, probably bringing in that rain Pete was talking about.

Pete and I help his wife climb up the rope. She calls me

"dear boy," and I respond with "ma'am." I feel the icy splash of raindrops—big, heavy ones—against my face.

Pete goes up next. He tells me he doesn't need any help, thank you very much.

Soon I am the last one standing in the driveway. I holster my gun, grab the ladder, and look around before I climb. Everything is silent and still except the rain, which makes a slapping noise against the tree leaves and a thudding against the house.

To me, it isn't gloomy or depressing. The rain is clean, natural, and untouched by the virus. It's the only part of the world that I know will always remain the same. I tip my head back and let it coat my face.

Then I pull myself up the ladder, toward the dark square of the open window.

Melanie isn't there. She must be with her family, comforting them and explaining what happened. I continue quickly up the ladder. All I want is to be with them.

Looking up, I see Melanie stick her head out the window. I stop and stare at her. She winces at the cold sting of rain and touches a wet spot on her scalp, as if water falling from the sky is a new thing to her.

As always, though, we are on the same wavelength, and she responds to the touch of rainfall by leaning even farther out the window, head tipped back, eyes closed, shoulders thrown back to let the water coat her face.

She looks down at me, wearing a smile of pure contentment.

"Come up," she says with a wave.

I climb the rest of the way. Melanie takes my hand and pulls me into the warm, dry darkness on the other side.

EPILOGUE

According to published reports in regional newspapers like *Clean World Gazette*, *Farmer's Almanac*, and *Repairman Sam*, the last infected person in the U.S. died from a gunshot wound to the head February 14, 2029, in a small Nebraska town called Victoria Springs.

It happened on Valentine's Day.

Our love letter to the virus, signed by a bullet.

It took a whole decade for the majority of the infected to die out on their own, mostly from animal attacks and exposure. We got so good at hiding and protecting ourselves from the threat that the virus struggled those last ten years to find new hosts, and was virtually extinct by the time that last bullet was fired.

The last infected man—nicknamed "Mr. Valentine" by the press—was by then a mere skeleton. Naked and hairless, he weighed ninety pounds and was completely blind.

Two brothers who had been out photographing sandhill cranes found him inside their shed. He was sitting with his back against the wall, head and neck slumped as if he'd had enough.

The brothers snapped a few pictures and called their father—a forty-four-year-old liquor store owner named Colin Smythe—who killed the infected man with a .22 magnum round fired from an antique Smith & Wesson revolver.

A few more photos were snapped of the corpse before the Smythe family wrapped the body in a tarp and contacted the press. The rest is history.

THANKS to the training I received from my father, I lived long enough to see the human race prevail. I still wake up thinking his blood is on my hands, though. Maybe it always will be. When the dreams wake me, Melanie (who always wakes up, too) tells me the same thing:

"You freed him from his pain, Kip."

I always respond the same way. I kiss her and tell her she freed me too, from a life without hope. She gave me a reason to live. I don't put it so eloquently, but the message gets across. Usually, our bodies do the rest of the talking, drawing on whatever energy we have left from long, hard days of fortifying Brightrock, so our children will always have somewhere to live.

As for my hometown, I'm not sure how it stands today. I've only been back twice: once to bury my father and again out of pure nostalgia. The second time was years ago—ten years after my father's death, to be exact—and it looked pretty much the same.

I visited my old house. By then, a family of eight, with five children, had taken shelter inside. It didn't bother me and never has. But I can sure as hell picture Dad frowning at the thought of wild kids tearing up the place, the little hellions completely oblivious to its history, how its walls and roof protected my family for so long. I think Dad and I would agree, though, that their safety makes it worthwhile. It's not like he needs it anymore.

And neither do I. Brightrock is my home now, and the home of my children with Melanie.

Someday I'll go back again. I'll go when the town has been fully restored, it's quaint buildings painted anew, the bulbs in its streetlamps replaced, its well-dressed inhabitants living as if things had always been that way.

I'll take Melanie and our kids and I'll tell them the story of how she and I met, but I'll leave out the scary parts until they're older.

It's the least I can do. I owe it to Peltham Park to see it alive again before I die.

And Peltham Park owes it to me.

THE END.

ABOUT THE AUTHOR

Richard Denoncourt is the author of horror, fantasy, and science fiction. He studied English literature and political philosophy at Colgate University, after which he received an MFA in Fiction from The New School.

Sign up here to join the author's newsletter. You'll be the first to hear about new releases. Thanks again for your support!

Contact the Author at

http://www.rdenoncourt.com/